THE MAKING OF JURASSIC PARK

THE MAKING OF JURASSIC PARK

DON SHAY & JODY DUNCAN

BALLANTINE BOOKS · NEW YORK

TM & © 1993 Universal City Studios, Inc. & Amblin Entertainment, Inc. Licensed by MCA Publishing Rights, Inc., a Division of MCA, Inc. All rights reserved.

All rights reserved under International and Pan-American Copyright Conventions. Published in the United States by Ballantine Books, a division of Random House, Inc., New York, and simultaneously in Canada by Random House of Canada Limited, Toronto.

Library of Congress Catalog Card Number: 92-97314

ISBN: 0-345-38122-X

Cover and text design by Michaelis/Carpelis Design Associates

Artwork courtesy of:

John Bell
Murray Close
Tom Cranham
Stefan Dechant
Peter Iovino
Marty Kline
Dave Lowery
Craig Mullins
Mark "Crash" McCreery
David Negran
Dan Sweetman
Jim Teegarden

Manufactured in the United States of America

First Edition: June 1993

10 9 8 7 6 5 4 3 2 1

ACKNOWLEDGMENTS

Do you want it good or do you want it fast?

Judging from the many slapdash books on the making of popular motion pictures, the answer to that question is most often woefully apparent. So as writers who take their work seriously, we were heartened by early meetings with representatives of Amblin Entertainment, MCA Publishing and Ballantine Books, all of whom expressed a strong commitment to producing a book of substance and quality on the making of *Jurassic Park*. Nearly a year has passed, during which we have observed and chronicled that film from preproduction to postproduction, and we are still impressed.

Our initial thanks must go to Steven Spielberg and to all the members of his remarkable cast and crew who made themselves available to us in the midst of an extremely complex shoot. A special nod is further owed to associate producer Lata Ryan who was there for us at the beginning and there for us at the end. Our gratitude extends likewise to the Amblin marketing team of Marvin Levy and Kris Kelly—and to Bonnie Curtis for an especially crucial telephone linkup. Thanks also to unit publicist Marsha Robertson and to Murray Close whose still photography illustrates much of this volume.

Our final vote of thanks goes to Nancy Cushing-Jones of MCA Publishing for her commitment to the project and for her ability to make things happen, and to her associate Jennifer Sebree for liaison and tireless support.

Don Shay & Jody Duncan

CONTENTS

Two weeks into the production of Jurassic Park—*on September 4, 1992—the Associated Press wire service carried the following news story:*

SAN FRANCISCO (AP)—A team of California scientists has cloned a fragment of genetic material from an extinct stingless bee that has been preserved in amber more than 25 million years.

The researchers, who extracted some of the insect's DNA and determined its exact molecular sequence, are attempting the new procedure on other amber-trapped ancient animals such as lizards, weevils and a biting midge that may have eaten dinosaur blood.

If the midge consumed dinosaur blood, the researchers said they may be able to unlock the secrets of the mysterious extinct reptiles and their evolution.

The report on the first stage of the scientists' work is being published in the current issue of the British journal *Medical Science Research* by Raul J. Cano, a molecular biologist at California Polytechnic State University in San Luis Obispo, Calif., and entomologist George O. Poinar Jr. of the University of California's College of Natural Resources in Berkeley.

While the research seems to echo *Jurassic Park*, the novel about scientists who bring dinosaurs back to life by cloning their DNA, Poinar said the real purpose of the experiment is to prove that it is possible to extract viable DNA from extinct animals and to seek firm new lines of evidence for an "evolutionary clock" that shows the pace of evolution over geologic time.

In the report published this week, the researchers describe how they were able to extract bits of muscle tissue from the wings of four of the bees whose bodies were preserved virtually intact in the resinous sap of an extinct tree.

The sap became amber as it solidified over hundreds of years. Poinar has collected insects and the fur of animals found in a mine in the Dominican Republic, where the trees lived 25 million to 40 million years ago.

Poinar's son Hendrik, a Cal Poly graduate student, and David W. Roubik, a Smithsonian Institution bee expert from Panama, are also part of the team.

The bee used in the experiment was a member of the species *Propledia dominicana,* an extinct ancestor of tropical stingless bees that bite rather than sting and that are widespread throughout the world today.

The sequencing of the ancient DNA shows that about 7 percent of the bee's original genetic material has changed in contemporary bees—a valuable clue to the rate at which evolution of the bees has progressed, Cano and Poinar said.

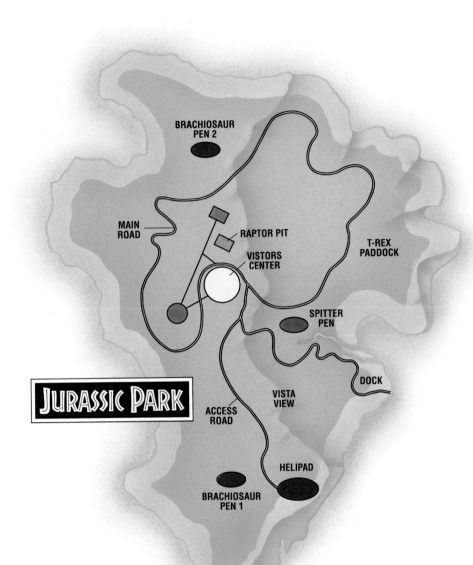

BRACHIOSAUR
PEN 2

MAIN
ROAD

RAPTOR PIT

VISTORS
CENTER

T-REX
PADDOCK

SPITTER
PEN

DOCK

JURASSIC PARK

VISTA
VIEW

ACCESS
ROAD

HELIPAD

BRACHIOSAUR
PEN 1

PART ONE

PRE-PRODUCTION

It was a union of intriguing possibilities.

One party was a bestselling writer of imaginative techno-fiction. The other was the world's most successful maker of films. Both had been greeted with celebrity at an early age; and both, after more than two decades of honing their respective skills, were in peak storytelling form.

Announced first in the motion picture trade journals, the news rippled quickly through the popular press and into the public consciousness. Michael Crichton had just completed his seventh novel, *Jurassic Park,* and Steven Spielberg was going to make it into a movie.

The title alone was enough to spark interest. Surely a book called *Jurassic Park* had to concern itself somehow with prehistoric animals. Michael Crichton was not about to disappoint. Though publication of the novel was still six months off, acknowledgment came early that its central theme was the cloning of dinosaurs for a futuristic theme park. Anyone familiar with Crichton's prior work—most especially *Westworld,* a 1971 film he both wrote and directed about robot characters running wildly amuck in a fantasyland resort—needed little imagination to speculate that all would not go as planned in the primordial park.

The core element of the novel had been germinating in Crichton's mind for nearly a decade. In 1981, he had, in fact, written an original screenplay centered on the notion of a genetically engineered dinosaur, but found it somehow wanting in execution. Unable to figure out how to fix it at the time, he set the script and the idea aside. A different approach occurred to him about three years later. "I resisted it at first. At the time there was a great dinosaur mania in this country; and I felt that if I did

Opposite: A color sketch of the *Jurassic Park* gateway as rendered by art director John Bell. *Below:* A foam carving, by Yarik Alfer, of the Jurassic Park logo.

something on dinosaurs, it would just be seen as part of a trend. I didn't particularly want that association, so I decided to wait. But the next year there was still a dinosaur mania and the year after that it was *still* going strong, so finally I realized that it was always going to be here." The turning point came in 1989. "My wife was pregnant with my first child, and I found that I couldn't walk past a toy store without buying a stuffed toy. And what I was buying, more often than not, were stuffed dinosaurs. My wife couldn't understand it. We knew we were having a girl. Why was I buying all these dinosaurs? And I would say, 'Well, girls like dinosaurs, too.' But it was clear that I was sort of obsessed with dinosaurs; and the whole idea of children and dinosaurs, and the meaning of what that was, was just on my mind a lot during that period."

Struck by the inevitability of it all, Crichton shifted his focus from stuffed dinosaurs to cloned dinosaurs and made the decision to resurrect his abandoned screenplay idea and develop it into a novel. A stickler for verisimilitude, he first had to develop a mechanism by which genetically engineered dinosaurs could be made viable in a bottom-line world. "Whenever I come up with an idea like extracting dinosaur DNA and then growing a new animal from it, what naturally occurs to me is, 'Well,

Above: Novelist Michael Crichton, producer Kathleen Kennedy, character creator Stan Winston and director Steven Spielberg pose with *King Kong* heroine Fay Wray on the *Jurassic Park* set. *Opposite:* To demonstrate his interest in the proposed film, Winston engaged his art department at Stan Winston Studio to produce dinosaur concepts long before the project was greenlighted. Pencil sketches of the triceratops, gallimimus, dilophosaur, parasaurolophus, velociraptor and brachiosaur were rendered by Mark "Crash" McCreery.

okay, who's going to pay for it?' The cost would most certainly be phenomenal—and what is it really worth to Stanford University to have a dinosaur? So part of the theme park idea had to do with how to pay for such a project. I actually resisted the notion because it seemed too much like *Westworld* and some of my other early ideas. But I couldn't think of any other way to pay for it. I still can't. I think if dinosaurs ever *are* cloned, it will be done by somebody for entertainment. And that fit in with another thing that interested me very much, which is the commercialization of genetic engineering—which is, I think, a very serious problem and one that we are still not facing. The fact that these dinosaurs are made for a park, it seemed to me, emphasized rather nicely the idea that all this amazing technology is being used for essentially commercial and frivolous purposes."

Once the necessity of a theme park was accepted, Crichton selected as its site a remote island off the west coast of Costa Rica. As the novel begins, the Jurassic Park project is nearing completion after six years of intense research and development under the utmost secrecy. Using dinosaur DNA extracted from the remains of blood-gorged mosquitos preserved in amber, a team of advanced bioengineers has succeeded in cloning fifteen different species of dinosaurs—some two hundred animals in all—which wealthy entrepreneur John Hammond envisions as the patentable attractions of his ultimate theme park. Summoned to the island to evaluate the progress are two renowned paleontologists, Alan Grant and Ellie Sattler, and a skeptical mathematician, expert in chaos theory, Ian Malcolm.

Begun during his wife's pregnancy, but not completed until well after, the first draft of *Jurassic Park* reflected Crichton's infatuation with the notion of dinosaurs as seen through the eyes of children—in this case, Hammond's two young grandchildren, Tim and Alexis Murphy, who are visiting the still top-secret resort while their parents sort out divorce issues. "The first draft was really told from the point of view of the children—and everyone who read it agreed that it was not entirely unsuccessful. I think it had to do with the idea that the fantasy of being among dinosaurs, of having dinosaurs once more in the world so that people could be with them was such an interesting fantasy that readers didn't want to experience it from the point of view of a child or an adolescent. They wanted an adult point of view. So the first change was to make it from the point of view of Grant—or mostly from that. The second major change was the addition of a tremendous amount of material on chaos

Crash McCreery at work on the gallimimus design. Both the book and film embraced recent paleontological theories that suggest an evolutionary link between dinosaurs and modern-day birds.

from this relatively minor, until that time, character of Malcolm. It was one of those things that writers describe, where I would be sitting at the typewriter and think, 'Well, it's time for Malcolm to say something,' and he would talk for three pages. And I would think, 'Well, that's funny, I was thinking more of three sentences.' And the next time he got a chance to talk the same thing would happen." Whatever the mechanism, it is readily apparent that Ian Malcolm—who pontificates insistently about the folly of creating and controlling nature—speaks largely with Crichton's voice. "Malcolm is very extreme, so I don't know that I would express myself exactly in his words. But the general sentiment, I think, is completely correct, that science is in many ways over the top, particularly in its arrogance."

The art department conceptualized the film working from galleys of the yet-to-be published book. *Left:* Among the concepts were David Negron and Tom Cranham renderings of the park environment. *Below:* An early John Bell costume sketch for John Hammond, the mastermind behind Jurassic Park.

TRICERATOPS

BRACHIOSAURUS

VELOCIRAPTOR

TYRANNOSAURUS REX

DILOPHOSAURUS

After additional rewrites and more than two years of work, Crichton delivered the *Jurassic Park* manuscript to his longtime publisher, Alfred A. Knopf, in May 1990. Within days, it was circulating around Hollywood. An undisputed "hot property," it would normally have been offered to the highest bidder. But Crichton had been party to a major bidding frenzy in the late seventies when his novel *Congo*—only an idea at the time—was purchased by Twentieth Century Fox for a then astonishing $1 million. Ultimately, however, the film never went into production. More concerned that a movie version of *Jurassic Park* get made than that top dollar be extracted from the process, Crichton instructed his agent, Robert Bookman of Creative Artists Associates, to offer the film rights at a fixed price of $1.5 million so that he could assess whatever interest might arise with fiscal dispassion.

Crichton had, in fact, already committed in principle to Steven Spielberg. "It all started when Michael and I were working on a script of his that I had purchased called *E.R.*—Emergency Room," Spielberg recalled. "We were talking about changes in my office one day and I happened to ask him what he was working on, aside from this screenplay. He said he had just finished a book about dinosaurs, called *Jurassic Park*, and that it was being proofed by his publisher. I said, 'You know, I've had a fascination with dinosaurs all my life and I'd really love to read it.' So he slipped me a copy of the galleys; and I read them and I called him the next day, and said, 'There's going to be a real hot bidding war for this, I'm sure.' But Michael said he wasn't really interested in getting into a bidding war. He wanted to give it to someone who would make the movie. So I said, 'I'd like to make it.' And he said, 'You mean you want to pro-

duce it or direct it?' I said, 'Both.' And he said, 'I'll give it to you if you guarantee me that you'll direct the picture.' But then the agency got ahold of it; and they, of course, encouraged a bidding war, even though Michael had kind of promised me the book privately. Before long, it had been sent out to every studio in town, and the bidding was fast and furious."

Offers flooded in immediately. "I was in Canada visiting," Crichton recalled, "and all these bids and negotiations were taking place. I was a very popular person in Hollywood—for about a day." The field was quickly narrowed to four serious contenders—each a big-time director with major studio backing. Twentieth Century Fox was pursuing the project for Joe Dante. Warner Brothers wanted it for Tim Burton. Guber-Peters Entertainment, in affiliation with TriStar Pictures, had Richard Donner in their corner. And Universal Pictures was pushing hard on behalf of Steven Spielberg. From his vacation retreat, Crichton spoke to all of them on the phone and ultimately reaffirmed his earlier predisposition based on whom he thought stood the best chance of actually getting the film made. Less than a week after it was offered for sale, a deal was locked and *Jurassic Park* was announced as a major motion picture to be directed by Steven Spielberg.

"I knew it was going to be a very difficult picture to make," observed Crichton. "Steven is arguably the most experienced and most successful

Opposite: Also on the design agenda was signage to identify individual dinosaur enclosures. John Bell conceived the signs as skeletal representations of the dinosaurs set against the backdrop of Isla Nublar, the island locale of Jurassic Park. / The park's most prominent structure was the visitor center, a multilevel building which housed the control room, hatchery and laboratory, as well as a central rotunda with fossilized exhibits from the Jurassic era. An early concept for the center by Tom Cranham. *Above:* A Craig Mullens illustration for a major sequence in which the tyrannosaurus rex escapes from her paddock and launches an attack on two stalled tour vehicles.

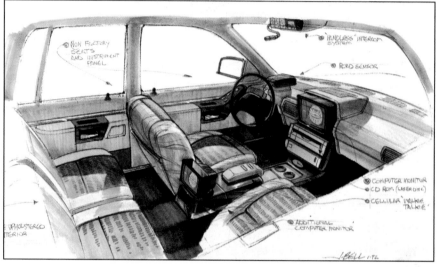

In addition to conceptualizing major sequences and park facilities, the art department had to concern itself with devising countless props and accessories, such as maintenance vehicles, tour cars and night vision goggles.

director of these kinds of movies. And he's really terrific at running the technology rather than letting the technology run him." Though delighted that Spielberg would be bringing his novel to the screen, Crichton had mixed feelings about the additional $500,000 he was offered to write the script. "From my point of view, I'd been lifting weights in my little office for however many years it was, trying to do an extremely difficult thing—which was to make a dinosaur story that really worked, that wasn't *One Million Years B.C.* And I finally thought I had something. But I was *so* tired of the whole area that I didn't really want to do the screenplay. I was sick of Malcolm and I was sick of Grant—and I was even sick of the dinosaurs. But I really felt that I knew the dimensions of the story. It was like a boat. Pull one part out and the water starts rushing in. Oops, don't do that! Do something else and the boat starts sailing too fast or in the wrong direction. I had already made a lot of those mistakes in my earlier drafts and I felt I knew the pitfalls. So I told Steven, 'I'll do a draft for you and cut it down to budgetable size; but then you're going to want somebody else to polish the characters.' I think that sort of surprised him, because writers never say, 'Get somebody else.'"

The task proved more daunting than even the weary Crichton had imagined. After some preliminary meetings to identify what Spielberg liked best and least about the book, the writer set about scaling his novel down to motion picture size. Seven months later, and only a few weeks after the book had at last been published and skyrocketed onto the best-seller list, he turned in his first draft. "Nobody was happy with it at all," Crichton recalled, "but Steven was great about it and he was really good at identifying what was wrong. I remember he said, 'The movie starts too fast.' And as soon as he said it, I knew he was right. It needed some version of what I had put in the book—a wind-up before the pitch—but I had gone right to the action and it didn't work. Then Steven suggested that we do it in forty-page chunks. I wrote the first one in about a month and we met and sort of adjusted it—but it was clearly in the right direction. People were happy now and I had a sense of that. There were story-boards and sketches and stuff immediately—within weeks after he

A David Negron painting depicting Alan Grant—one of three scientists summoned to conduct an inspection of the park—fleeing from the escaped T-rex in the company of Hammond's terrified grandchildren, Tim and Alexis Murphy. Based on descriptions taken directly from the Crichton novel, such preproduction renderings proved invaluable in developing the eventual storyline for the film.

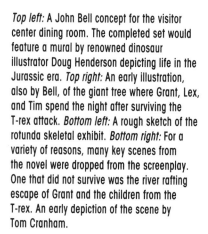

Top left: A John Bell concept for the visitor center dining room. The completed set would feature a mural by renowned dinosaur illustrator Doug Henderson depicting life in the Jurassic era. *Top right:* An early illustration, also by Bell, of the giant tree where Grant, Lex, and Tim spend the night after surviving the T-rex attack. *Bottom left:* A rough sketch of the rotunda skeletal exhibit. *Bottom right:* For a variety of reasons, many key scenes from the novel were dropped from the screenplay. One that did not survive was the river rafting escape of Grant and the children from the T-rex. An early depiction of the scene by Tom Cranham.

acquired the book—and so I was able to do a lot of writing from those. I turned the second chunk in about a month later and the final one in about two months after that. It was hard for me to do, but it was a really good experience. Steven was amazing to work with—intelligent and sane—not at all like the movie business."

Signed on to produce the film was Kathleen Kennedy, whose fourteen-year association with Spielberg had begun with a modest production assistant role on *1941*. In successive years, she had advanced to associate producer and producer; and in 1984, had founded Amblin Entertainment with Spielberg and fellow producer, later husband, Frank Marshall. Sharing the producing credit on *Jurassic Park* would be Gerald R. Molen, who had earlier worked with Amblin in a unit production manager and

associate producer capacity. Serving as associate producer on the picture would be Lata Ryan.

Left: Among the earliest to join the *Jurassic Park* creative team was production designer Rick Carter. *Right:* Carter confers with art director Jim Teegarden.

For a film that would require not only an exotic setting, but also a host of enormous prehistoric beasts, it was evident that bringing an accomplished production designer onto the project at the earliest opportunity would be a decided advantage. Without hesitation, Spielberg selected Rick Carter. As a young production designer on Spielberg's venture into episodic television, *Amazing Stories,* Carter had designed every show, including two of the director's own. "Rick did all forty-four episodes of *Amazing Stories,*" observed Spielberg, "which was like going to college for two years and getting on-the-job training. I loved what he did. To do an anthology series where every single show had a different concept was like being forty-four different production designers on feature-looking episodes. I thought Rick could do anything asked of him. He has no boundaries, no single style. He is the chameleon of production designers in Hollywood today." After his stint on *Amazing Stories,* Carter had done some late work on *Empire of the Sun* and had devoted several weeks to *Rain Man* at a time when Spielberg anticipated directing it. Under the Amblin banner, he had also designed the final two entries in the *Back to the Future* trilogy for director Robert Zemeckis.

"I was brought onto *Jurassic Park* about two years before we finally started shooting," Carter observed. "At the time, the only other people involved were Steven, the producers, and Michael Crichton. The script had not been written—we were working from galleys of the book—so for me, it was a great opportunity to be able to actually help shape the

Left: Engaged originally to help conceptualize the film, assistant art director Marty Kline would later design the jungle settings constructed on studio sound stages. *Right:* John Bell at work in the Amblin art department. *Below:* Security badges worn by Jurassic Park visitors and staff.

film. On most shows, the production designer is brought in and handed a script and asked to visualize it. Not so on this one. I was in on many early meetings with Steven where we would break down the scenes in the book and discuss which ones would work best for the film."

"Believe it or not," said Spielberg, "the first thing I thought was that the book had too many dinosaurs in it. I didn't think it was physically possible to make a movie that chock-full of dinosaurs. But Michael had done a wonderful job on the book, both from the scientific perspective and from the adventure side. His best accomplishment, I think, was creating a basis of credibility that dinosaurs could return to the living today and walk amongst us. He had set up the logic and feasibility of such an occurrence. What I wanted to do was boil the book down and choose my seven or eight favorite scenes and base the script around those. So we crunched the book."

A number of conceptual illustrators and storyboard artists were enlisted to help focus the rich visual imagery of the novel into something that could be translated onto film. Among them was Marty Kline. "There were four of us doing storyboards," said Kline, "Ed Verreaux, Tom Cranham, Dave Lowery, and myself. John Bell was illustrating sequences that involved a lot of design because he is a very strong designer. Then we had Dave Negron and Craig Mullins doing full-blown paintings of some major scenes. So there were quite a few of us involved. We began working from the galleys, because at that point the book had not even been published yet. We were just taking sequences and storyboarding what we read—which was not particularly difficult since

Left: A John Bell depiction of the massive electrified fence surrounding the tyrannosaur paddock. *Below:* In the story, the fence is deactivated when the park's power systems are disengaged, enabling the T-rex to tear through the towering structure and assault the tour vehicles stalled outside. An early sketch of the attack by Bell.

Michael Crichton writes a mix of action and technology and the book was very visual. Rick was developing scenes—the attack of the T-rex and the escape down the river—and we were storyboarding them. Then Rick would propose them to Steven, and Steven would respond—often with his own little thumbnail sketches. Our approach was very broad at first, but soon we began throwing things out and focusing on what Steven really wanted to see. In the process, a lot of major sequences were cut. We cut the sequence of the pterosaurs in the aviary pretty early because it didn't seem to be pulling the plot along; and much later the whole river raft sequence, which became enormous, logistically and cinematically, was also lost. A lot of tough choices had to be made."

The behavioral character of the dinosaurs was an issue that concerned everyone on the creative team. "What we tried to do," said Carter, "was find the animal in the dinosaur as opposed to the monster in the dinosaur. The idea was not to make them any less threatening, but rather to keep them from doing as much monster 'schtick.' For our human characters, we wanted their situation to be more like they were being stalked by an animal that is a carnivore, as opposed to something that is psychopathic and just out to get them. That's one of the reasons we wanted to have herds of dinosaurs, to show that dinosaurs were just like any other life-form and that they lived out their lives in a somewhat naturalistic manner."

Spielberg had his own personal favorites among the generally hackneyed dinosaur movies he had embraced as a youth. "Most of them were

Opposite: Inside the park laboratory, a team of genetic engineers has successfully cloned long-extinct dinosaurs using DNA extracted from Jurassic era mosquitos trapped in amber. John Bell concept sketches of lab equipment featured variations of the embryo storage unit and the egg hatchery. *This page:* Other Bell sketches included Hammond's corporate helicopter, the amber mine featured early in the film, and a taser gun employed by the raptor guards.

awful, but each one had some good parts. *Gorgo* had the mama dinosaur coming after her baby who was stuck in a circus. *The Beast from 20,000 Fathoms* was a really good yarn with some great architectural destruction. *Godzilla,* of course, was the most masterful of all the dinosaur movies because it made you believe it was really happening." But for *Jurassic Park,* Spielberg was looking for something altogether different. "I never thought I wanted to do a dinosaur movie better than anyone else's, but I did want my dinosaur movie to be the most realistic of them all. I wanted the audience to say, 'I really believe this could happen today.' *Close Encounters,* in a way, was based on both scientific and popular belief that UFOs have existed—or at the very least, *could* exist. And there was a credibility in that film that I drew upon in attacking *Jurassic Park.* I wanted my dinosaurs to be animals. I wouldn't even let anyone call them monsters or creatures. What I was after was kind of like *Nova* meets *Explorer,* with a little bit of *Raiders of the Lost Ark* and *Jaws* mixed in. But if I had to aspire to a particular movie, it would be *Hatari.* To me, that was the high-water mark of man versus the natural in a feature film."

As the book narrative progressed into screenplay form, Crichton's fifteen animal species were winnowed down to a more manageable seven. Exactly how they would be brought into being, however, was a matter of some debate. Traditionally, dinosaur movies have been achieved most successfully with some variation of stop-motion animation, a process whereby an armatured puppet is animated in tiny increments and photographed one frame at a time to simulate natural movement. From a director's perspective, the disadvantage to this approach is that much of the essential action is relegated to postproduction effects artisans. "Steven was not enthusiastic about using miniature puppets," Carter recalled. "He wanted to have as much full-scale as he could pull off so that he could convey what it would be like to be in the same time and space as the dinosaur. That way, he would be much more fluid with his camera in relationship to the dinosaurs—which is his style of filmmaking. That isn't to say that he hasn't done a lot of special effects movies where people are talking to nothing or looking at nothing; but in this case, to have something there on the set was important. That was going to be the power of the film—to see how well the dinosaurs came across

Another scene, illustrated by John Bell but ultimately dropped from the film, was one in which Lex has a playful encounter with a baby triceratops. Not contained in Crichton's novel, the sequence had been conceived as a mechanism for revealing some of the resident dinosaurs' more benign characteristics.

Above: Among the most ferocious of the park inhabitants are the velociraptors, highly intelligent predators that are isolated and contained within a closely guarded enclosure. A Tom Cranham sketch of the raptor pen. *Left:* Cranham also produced sketches of the visitor center rotunda featuring a skeletal display of a tyrannosaur and an alamosaur in mock battle.

as something you've never seen before. Steven had done that very effectively with *E.T.* and *Jaws*—both a benign and a ferocious animal. This was more like *Close Encounters of the Prehistoric Kind.*"

Since nearly every film Spielberg had made in the past decade had incorporated cinematic trickery by Industrial Light and Magic—founded by his old friend George Lucas to produce the revolutionary visual effects for *Star Wars*—Spielberg consulted early on with ILM effects supervisor Dennis Muren. A meticulous artist with six Academy Awards to his credit—two of them for the Spielberg films *E. T.* and *Indiana Jones and the Temple of Doom*—Muren was high on anyone's list of the best in the business. But despite the enormity of the *Jurassic Park* project, Muren felt initially that there would not be much in it that would appeal to him professionally. "At the time," Muren recalled, "Steven was pretty much insistent on doing it all with full-size robotic dinosaurs that he was going to have made. He had seen the 'King Kong' ride at the Universal Studios tour in Florida and thought it was fabulous. He felt that if somebody could do that, then with some more direction they could make dinosaurs that would be able to do most of what he needed for this film. So the dinosaurs were going to be these big, full-size mechanical robots; and ILM's part was going to be all the little stuff that was left."

Among the earliest players on the *Jurassic Park* team was physical effects supervisor Michael Lantieri—who had worked with Spielberg on *Indiana Jones and the Last Crusade* and with director Robert Zemeckis on other Amblin projects such as *Who Framed Roger Rabbit* and *Back to the Future II* and *III.* Together, they approached theme park engineer Robert Gurr of GurrDesign, Inc., who had built the mechanical King Kong that had so captivated Spielberg. Having produced a number of large-scale park attractions, Gurr felt confident that he could deliver a full-size tyrannosaurus rex that would satisfy the filmmakers, and set about drawing up plans. Although optimism ran high in both camps,

Concepts for the visitor center evolved considerably during the two-year design period. An early rendering by John Bell incorporated columns that resembled the graceful head and long neck of a brachiosaur.

Spielberg eventually became resigned to the fact that a fully convincing, twenty-foot-tall ambulatory dinosaur was beyond current robotics capabilities. Though he still wanted as much full-size dinosaur material as possible, he opted to shift his approach to more conventional filmmaking techniques.

Key among the potential candidates was character creator Stan Winston. Like many of his contemporaries, Winston had begun his career as a makeup effects artist working primarily with transformative foam latex appliances affixed to actors' faces and figures. Then as science fiction and fantasy films became more imaginatively conceived, he joined other leaders in the field by expanding into partially and even fully mechanical creations to satisfy the demands of writers and directors obsessed with pushing the boundaries of cinematic illusion. His work with director James Cameron on *The Terminator* and *Aliens* had earned him kudos and a visual effects Oscar, and he was again collaborating with Cameron on *Terminator 2* when Kathy Kennedy called to talk about *Jurassic Park* in December 1990.

"At that point," said Winston, "there was still question about whether there was going to be a *Jurassic Park*, whether it could be done for a budget. Everybody at my studio wanted to do the film—we're all major dinosaur fans—and I had always wanted to work with Steven. So it was a matter, to some extent, of going for the job." Even though the project

A color sketch by John Bell—produced before the storyline had been finalized—illustrating a briefly considered ending in which John Hammond is left behind on Isla Nublar as the remaining park survivors depart via helicopter.

had not yet been greenlighted, Winston pulled his premier conceptual artist, Mark "Crash" McCreery, off all other assignments and put him to work rendering detailed pencil sketches of key dinosaurs featured in the book. "The initial drawings were on me. There was no deal, there were no dollars from Universal or Amblin. It was like a good faith thing to show that we had real interest in the project. Also, since it was questionable whether the project was going to go forward, it seemed to me that these drawings and any development we did on the dinosaurs would give the studio executives something to look at and get excited about, and hopefully that would generate some momentum."

McCreery's first drawing was a motion study of a tyrannosaur running against a plain white background. His second revealed the beast in a jungle setting with its left leg raised high in an attack mode suggestive of a bird of prey. "I wanted to get as far away from people's perceptions of dinosaurs as possible," said McCreery, "the upright, bulky, clumsy kinds of creatures that have been seen in previous movies. The idea was

All of the park inhabitants were designed at Stan Winston Studio. Winston illustrator Crash McCreery produced a series of dinosaur sketches and motion studies, including a tyrannosaurus rex poised for attack. Unlike the lumbering lizards seen in previous dinosaur movies, the *Jurassic Park* dinsosaurs were depicted as agile, warm-blooded animals.

Crash McCreery sketches of the velociraptor adults and hatchling. While allowing minor concessions to dramatic necessity, the Winston design team adhered to scientific authority as much as possible in developing their dinosaurs.

to show that we were up-do-date on the current thinking that dinosaurs were probably warm-blooded and birdlike rather cold-blooded and lizardlike. There was nothing in the drawings that had to do specifically with *Jurassic Park*. Stan just wanted to be able to show Steven that we were on top of things as far as what dinosaurs are supposed to look like." Working from anatomical breakdowns found in scholarly texts by respected paleontologists such as Robert Bakker and Gregory Paul, McCreery spent anywhere from two to four weeks on each rendering, working and reworking the forms and action until he was fully satisfied with the results.

His drawings produced exactly the results Winston had hoped for at both Amblin and Universal. "Everyone was very excited about the T-rex," Winston recalled, "so we said, 'Okay, let's start drawing the next character.' So Crash started sketching the velociraptor. Then, while we were shooting *Terminator 2,* I had Mike Trcic start sculpting a miniature T-rex. It was a kind of development process I had never done before. We didn't have a contract, didn't have a job—although after a while Universal did start paying me for the time my artists were putting in. There were constant rumors that *Jurassic Park* was not going to get made or that Steven had decided not to do it. Through it all, we just kept plodding forward, hoping to make the picture happen both for us and for the studio."

Before too many months had elapsed, it became evident that *Jurassic Park* would need much more than the usual production in terms of preparation. Much of it would have to be accomplished and proved practicable before the studio would even consider greenlighting the project. Key decision-makers were skeptical that full-size mechanical dinosaurs could be made to work convincingly. Memories still lingered of the fifty-foot mechanical ape producer Dino De Laurentiis had insisted upon for his *King Kong* remake that had cost more than a million dollars and performed so woodenly that it merited only about ten seconds of actual screen time. Kong was a definite setback, yet the allure of full-size creatures remained strong among filmmakers. "Any director wants to do as

After months of preliminary design work, the Winston organization began construction on a variety of animatronic dinosaurs, including a full-scale tyrannosaurus rex. To guide the sculptors with the full scale dinosaurs a preliminary ⅕ scale version was created.

much of his film live on set as possible," stated Winston. "It just makes sense. He would rather be working with his actors, directing them and seeing the scene as it is being shot rather than having to wait for someone to hand him an effects scene at some later date. So, naturally, Steven wanted to do as much full-size work as possible on *Jurassic Park*."

Winston had an advantage of sorts in that he had successfully built a fifteen-foot-tall alien queen for *Aliens* that had performed wonderfully. It was assumed that he stood a good chance of making a twenty-foot-tall tyrannosaur that could do likewise. Winston did nothing to discourage that notion, even though he knew full well that the technology needed to create a massive upright dinosaur would be vastly different from the rather spindly alien queen. By all estimates, the T-rex would be a five-thousand-pound animatronic robot that needed to perform with perfect fluidity.

After months of informal development, Universal finally entered into a contractual agreement with Stan Winston Studio to create the *Jurassic Park* dinosaurs, still hedging their bets by withholding an unconditional go-ahead for the overall production. It was evident to Spielberg that

Full size scaled blow-up of the original two-dimensional T-rex rendering.

Winston art department coordinator Shane Mahan finalizes the dilophosaur sculpture. Nicknamed the spitter, the fictionalized dilophosaur was a small, venom-spewing dinosaur with an expanding cowl that vibrated angrily as the animal prepared to attack.

his dinosaur picture still had a long way to go. So after setting the course for its preproduction effort, Spielberg retrimmed his sails and began work on *Hook,* his ambitious retelling of the Peter Pan fable starring Robin Williams and Dustin Hoffman. Engrossed in that film for nearly a year, Spielberg continued to monitor the progress of the *Jurassic Park* script and the ongoing work by his effects and design teams. Eventually, while Stan Winston and company continued to labor on their animatronic dinosaurs, even the art department took a virtual eight-month hiatus to design and construct the sets for *Death Becomes Her,* a black comedy by Robert Zemeckis.

As with most characters developed at Stan Winston Studio, responsibility for the *Jurassic Park* dinosaurs was divided between two separate, but closely linked entities within the company. The art department, overseen by coordinators Shane Mahan and John Rosengrant, was tasked with creating each dinosaur's outer form, while the mechanical department, under coordinators Richard Landon and Craig Caton, was charged with developing the internal mechanisms that would bring the beast to life. Recognizing that the scope of *Jurassic Park* far exceeded anything his studio had encountered to date, Winston instituted a further organizational breakdown, designating separate teams, comprised of both art department and mechanical department people, to shepherd each character through to completion.

The tyrannosaurus rex was obviously the most imposing project. A mold was made of the fifth-scale rex that had been sculpted during the early conceptual process. From it, a rigid foam casting was made and then sliced precisely into cross-sections. "It was like slicing a loaf of bread," observed Mahan. "Then each piece was numbered and put on an opaque projector and projected up five times onto a piece of plywood. The plywood pieces were cut out—reduced by two inches to allow for clay—and hooked onto a sculpting armature. That gave us a fair amount of proportion right there. We spanned that form with hardware cloth and fiberglass, and then put our clay on top of that. It was a really big construction—about twenty feet tall. We had eight or ten people sculpting on it every day and it took us about sixteen weeks to finish it." Some three thousand pounds of clay were required to complete the sculpture.

Creating the outer form of the T-rex, though daunting in scale, was reasonably straightforward and in keeping with established practices. The mechanisms required to activate it, however, were an entirely different matter. Most puppet characters are actuated through a combination of techniques. Full-body movements are often obtained by having one or more human performers inside the puppet, space and character configuration permitting. When that approach is prohibitive, rods and wires controlled externally by puppeteers are common alternatives. On particularly large puppets, hydraulic actuators are sometimes employed to provide the required muscle-power.

It was clear that hydraulics would be needed to actuate the gargantuan T-rex. The trick was finding a means of transforming the essentially mechanical movements thus produced into convincing simulations of

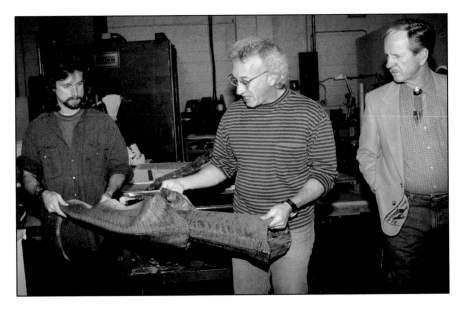

Art department coordinator John Rosengrant and Stan Winston demonstrate an initial skin and core test taken from the ⅕ scale T-rex for producer Gerald Molen. A variety of puppets, insert heads and legs, and raptor suits would be required to fully portray the man-size predators on film.

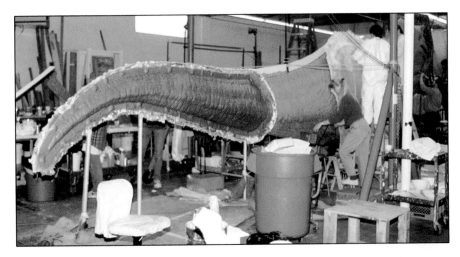

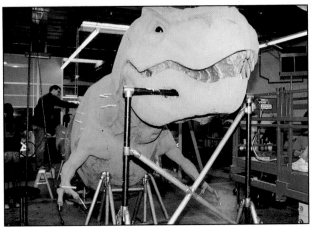

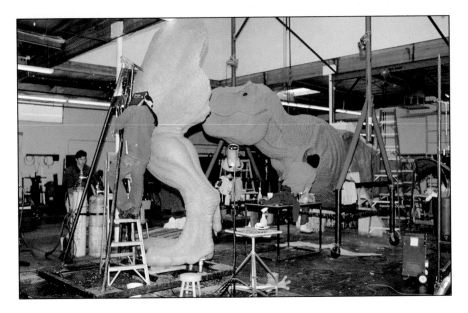

Opposite, clockwise: A Crash McCreery sketch of the tyrannosaurus rex. / Winston sculptors Mike Trcic, Joey Orosco, Mark Jurinko, Bill Basso, Robert Henderstien and Greg Fiegel at work on the full-size animal. / Len Burge details one of the feet. / Christopher Swift attends to an upper leg. / The fifth-scale maquette and its full-size counterpart. *This page, clockwise:* Marilyn Chaney, Mark Jurinko, Mike Trcic, Christopher Swift and Ian Stevenson prepare the completed sculpture for molding and casting. / The head and neck in progress. / Armando Gonzales at work on welding the T-rex leg armature support. / Trcic details the head.

Clockwise: While the art department realized the sculpting, molding, and painting of the T-rex, the Winston mechanical department was responsible for its complex electronic and hydraulic systems. To provide gross body movements, the massive animal was mounted on a motion platform akin to a flight simulator. / Key to the performance of the animatronic creation was a fifth-scale waldo which, through a computerized interface, was linked to the full-size rig, thereby enabling precise moves to be choreographed manually on the set. / McFadden Systems custom-built the hydraulic motion base.

muscular motivation—and tangentially to create and orchestrate specific organic action quickly and simply on stage. "The approach we ended up using came to me after visiting a robotic manufacturer that does a lot of work for Disneyland and Disney World," said Winston. "We were there to talk to them about their hydraulic cylinders and actuating devices. During the visit, I put on one of their telemetry suits." A telemetry suit is a device that electronically links a human controller to a robotic figure, so that any movement the controller makes while wearing the suit is replicated, almost instantly, by his robot counterpart. "In the middle of the night I woke up with the idea of creating a small T-rex puppet that would link to our full-size one so that every axis of movement would be covered—about forty of them in all. With four puppeteers we could move the small puppet around manually, and every movement would be translated to the hydraulics and duplicated by the big dinosaur."

Once it was established that the Stan Winston tyrannosaur would be used for relatively tight shots, the decision was made to split the dinosaur in two. The upper portion would include the head and torso and tail, and would be mounted on a customized flight simulator platform. "Craig Caton came up with the concept," said Winston. "Flight simulators are, after all, a proven commodity. What they do is take big heavy objects and move them around smoothly with force and strength and speed. The minute it was suggested, it was like, 'Of course!' I immediately went to Steven and told him we had this great idea. We knew it was going to be expensive, but everybody agreed it was the way to go." Much of the basic platform construction was contracted out to McFadden Systems, a manufacturer of simulator platforms for the aircraft industry. "The mechanism was based on a flight simulator, but it's not a flight simulator—it's a 'dino simulator.' It was built specifically for us, to our dimensions for this T-rex. But the concept is the same. We took all this hydraulic technology and spread it up through the simulator, into the body, out to the tip of the tail and the tip of the head."

"There are actually two platforms," noted Richard Landon. "The lower mounts to the ground—in our case, a pit on the stage—and the

Above: Hydraulics engineer Lloyd Ball and Eric Ostroff adjust the mechanisms on the T-rex walking legs, a separate construct designed to complement the simulator-based upper portion of the dinosaur. *Below:* Mechanical department crew members Alan Scott and Tony McCray at work on the internal rigging for the head and torso assembly.

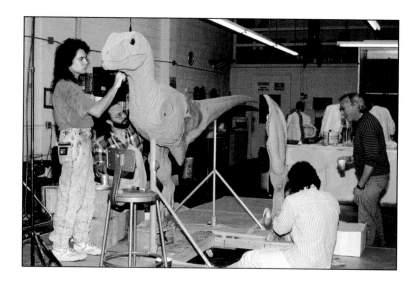

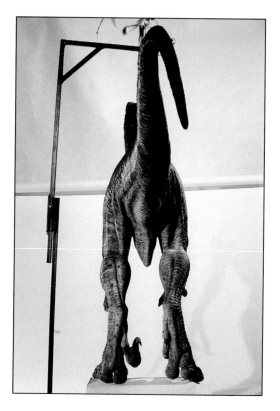

other mounts to the flight simulator or creature or whatever. Ours had a full six axes of motion. It could move up and down, front to back, left to right, pitch left to right, rock front to back. It had complete motion. Both the platform and the T-rex were hydraulically actuated—even the facial functions—and everything ran through a computer control board. Only the eyes were radio controlled." While the giant hydraulic armature was being constructed, a fifth-scale version was fabricated so that its axes of motion could be interlocked with the big one via the computer. Motion in the full-size T-rex could then be produced by manually moving the scaled-down armature into desired positions. "It was almost like sculpting motion rather than sculpting clay. We could readily put the big T-rex through its paces by moving the miniature motion base and by puppeteering the small armature manually." Though the moves would be generated manually, the computer interfacing the large- and small-scale puppets was able to record the moves for precise replaying of approved choreography.

While the dino simulator would be used for all up-angles on the beast, other shots required that the legs be seen meeting the ground. Constructed for this purpose was a rolling platform upon which the T-rex underbelly was mounted with hydraulic legs and tail attached. Also constructed was a separate T-rex head with extra detailing and added mechanics for closeup photography.

Throughout the development phase, Winston and his team collaborated closely with Michael Lantieri, whose physical effects rigging would intersect often with their work. "This was the first movie I had done where there was no clear-cut separation between the various effects teams," said Lantieri. "We knew that Stan was one of the best creature people around, if not *the* best, so there was no doubt that he could build the dinosaurs and create all the facial movements and other articulations. The thing about this film, though, was that there was some big, heavy stuff that had to be moved around with great agility. So that's where we all worked together. Stan and his people would build the skins and all the mechanisms underneath, and we would build the exterior cranes and the large-scale hydraulics to support and move them around." Even the simulator platform for the T-rex would wind up sitting on a pneumatic motion base built by the physical effects team to facilitate its repositioning on the stage.

Although the tyrannosaur was the most challenging creation for the Stan Winston team, it was by no means the only prehistoric beast on the

Stan Winston Studio also designed and fabricated a variety of animatronic velociraptors. Among them were full-sized, cable-actuated puppets, a counterweighted, fully actuated raptor head, insert legs, and a pair of raptor suits worn by human performers. *Opposite, clockwise from upper left:* Christopher Swift, Joe Reader and Mark Jurinko sculpt the full-scale raptor as Stan Winston observes. / Nonarticulated, but posable, raptor puppets were constructed primarily as on set lighting stand-ins, for live action puppet work and C.G. / The fully animatronic raptor head used for closeups. A side view of the posable raptor puppet.

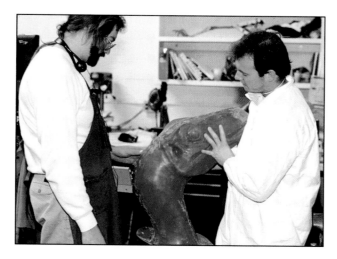

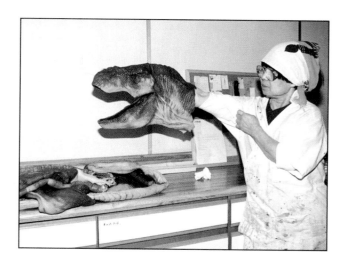

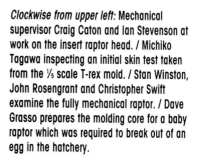

Clockwise from upper left: Mechanical supervisor Craig Caton and Ian Stevenson at work on the insert raptor head. / Michiko Tagawa inspecting an initial skin test taken from the ⅕ scale T-rex mold. / Stan Winston, John Rosengrant and Christopher Swift examine the fully mechanical raptor. / Dave Grasso prepares the molding core for a baby raptor which was required to break out of an egg in the hatchery.

docket. At least as prominent in both the novel and the screenplay was the velociraptor, a roughly human-size predator of great ferocity. As presented in the book, the velociraptor is an efficient pack hunter, cunning and intelligent. "The raptor was one of the major characters in the story," said John Rosengrant, "and because of how energetic it is, it needed the most options from a puppeteering point of view. We went with both high-tech and low-tech approaches. The low-tech approach was to build a suit that a human operator—me, in most cases—could wear. It's always an advantage to have a people-powered character because of the range of movements the human operator can produce. Even our low-tech suit, however, was loaded with nifty radio control mechanisms for the eyes;

and the tiny arms were half cable-operated and half radio-controlled." Since the raptor's legs were triple-jointed—like the hind legs of a dog— the plan was to use the suit for shots showing the creature from the knees up. The balancing tail was to be articulated externally via concealed rods and wires.

Also constructed was a full, mechanical puppet capable of being supported by a variety of rigs, most extending down through the set floors which would be elevated off the stages specifically to accommodate the needs of the creature crew. "The full puppet really produced the strongest and most dynamic motion," Rosengrant continued. "The suit was great for broad body-English types of moves and it had some good

Clockwise from upper left: One of the two in-progress raptor suits fashioned for the film. / Craig Caton at work on the cable mechanisms for the raptor insert head. / An early sketch illustrating the performer's position inside the suit. / Another view of the raptor suit under construction.

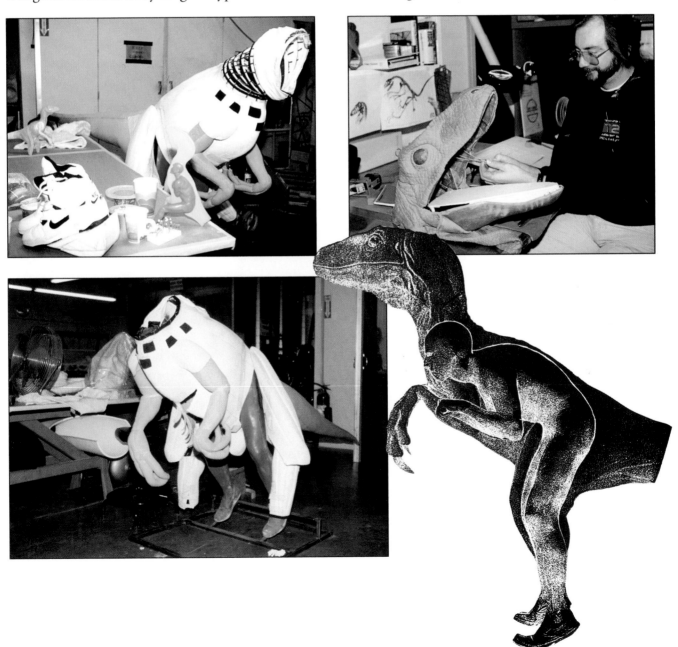

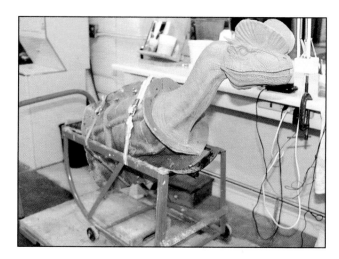

For the spitter, a full-size body puppet was constructed and employed in tandem with three separate heads, each of which performed a different function. *Top left:* Dave Grasso sculpts a fifth-scale prototype. *Top right:* A completed mold for the full-size spitter. *Below:* Rick Galinson, who engineered the spitter mechanics, adjusts the puppet's cable control system.

head movement; but the puppet, being cable-powered with nicely machined mechanics inside, could really spin its head around and get some compound, organic moves. That was its forte."

Other variations were developed to meet specific requirements. "As the storyboards started coming in, we realized there was a real need to see the lower part of the animal as the raptor is stalking around and creeping in on people. So we made a walking rig that was three-quarters of the animal—from about its neck down—and I would be popping out of the middle of it. There were feet extensions on the legs and I would be suspended from above so there was just enough weight on my feet to allow me to feel where I was going. The arms on the creature were radio controlled and the toes were cable operated. So I would provide the leg movement, but the forward motion was created by members of the crew pushing on the rig and the toes were operated by other puppeteers."

Among the most involved of the raptor rigs was a device developed to create fluid movement for a highly detailed head and neck assembly built for closeup shots. The mechanism was actually an offshoot of work being done on yet another prehistoric predator, the four-foot-tall dilophosaur, which Michael Crichton conceived as having the ability to spit venom into the eyes of its prey. "The idea was proposed first for the raptor," said Winston, "but no one was convinced that it would work on anything that large. So we decided to try it out on the spitter." The springboard for the concept was the industry-standard Steadicam system, a counter-weighted device that essentially renders motion-picture cameras neutrally buoyant so that they can be hand-held with ease and operated with great fluidity. "Although the technology had been there for years, it had never been used in our kind of work. Rick Galinson started developing this concept for the spitter and the results were stunning. The moves were incredibly smooth and organic—to the point where it was the most perfect cable-controlled creature I had ever seen. At that point, I scrapped an alternate approach we were taking on the raptor insert head and reapplied the same technique. Fortunately, it worked just as well on the larger animal."

The dilophosaurus represented the film's only serious departure from scientific veracity. In actuality, the beast had stood about ten feet tall; but

Above: Rick Galinson operating the spitter controls. *Below:* Associate producer Lata Ryan, cast member Richard Attenborough and Stan Winston inspect the full-size spitter in progress. Ryan, who came onto the *Jurassic Park* project in September 1990 to oversee the initial design effort, was one of the original members of the production team.

for movie purposes, and to avoid confusion with the velociraptors, it was decided to make it about four feet tall instead. The creature's ability to spit venom was a Crichton fabrication; but true to its real-life counterpart, its head sported a bony V-shaped crest. Added by the production art department was an interesting feature. When the dilophosaur prepared to spit, a fanlike hood, normally folded back against its neck, would flare out around its head in the manner of an Australian frilled lizard. The dilophosaur team, headed by Shane Mahan, bypassed the customary practice of sculpting a miniature and then scaling it up to full size. "I felt confident that we didn't need to do a maquette first," Mahan remarked, "and I wanted to get right into the actual character. There were four of us working on it. I would block out an area and sketch in the detail, and the others would come in and do the finishing work." Three separate heads were required to produce the various actions called for in the script.

Although Spielberg hoped to get as much dinosaur footage "live" on stage as possible, he recognized that certain types of shots—such as full-

Above: Crash McCreery applies paint to the fully articulated raptor puppet. *Right:* The completed posable raptor. *Below:* Christopher Swift covers the animatronic raptor with its foam latex skin.

Left: Shane Mahan designed and applied the spitter color scheme over Crash McCreery's initial pencil drawing. *Below:* The completed fifth-scale prototype.

length views of the T-rex walking—would have to be obtained through some form of miniature photography. In the early years of silent moviemaking, Willis O'Brien had pioneered a means of photographing dinosaur puppets via stop-motion puppet animation. Though refinements were made over the years—most notably by O'Brien protegé and successor Ray Harryhausen—the technique had remained substantially unchanged until a decade ago when Industrial Light and Magic developed an experiment employed in *The Empire Strikes Back* into a full-blown innovation on *Dragonslayer.* By using motion control technology, which had swept through the effects business in the wake of *Star Wars,* technicians at ILM developed puppet characters with rods extending from their extremities that could be attached to computer-controlled stepper motors. Thus, the principal puppet articulations which had been painstakingly produced by stop-motion animators for decades could now be stored in computer memory and repeated—with modifications, if desired. Most significantly, the use of motion control allowed the puppet to blur slightly from frame to frame, thereby eliminating the occasional strobing effect characteristic of stop-motion and considered objectionable by some. Though traditionalists found the high-tech approach cumbersome and unnecessary, go-motion animation, as it was dubbed by its proponents, had gradually won recognition as a means of producing more fluid and convincing puppet photography.

Phil Tippett, an Academy Award winner for *Return of the Jedi,* had been the principal animator on *Dragonslayer.* In ensuing years, both at ILM and later at his own Tippett Studio, he had perfected go-motion as a viable effects methodology. Known as an exceptional artist and a major dinosaur enthusiast, Tippett was approached by Amblin early on, but had shied away from *Jurassic Park* when he learned of Spielberg's plans to use robot dinosaurs. Later, with Stan Winston on the project and ILM in the wings, his interest was regenerated. With only a modicum of additional coaxing, Tippett agreed to put together a team to supply the fifty or so go-motion puppet shots it was anticipated would be needed to expand upon the Stan Winston material.

An acknowledged authority on animal behavior and movement, Tippett was charged first with producing some test footage that could be used by the Winston team to suggest the kinds of moves their full-size dinosaurs would need to make. Working from maquettes provided by Winston, Tippett and company built armatured puppets and employed traditional stop-motion to animate them. "We used a fifth-scale model of the raptors and a sixteenth-scale T-rex," Tippett explained. "I laid out a scenario for some motion tests and went through a number of permu-

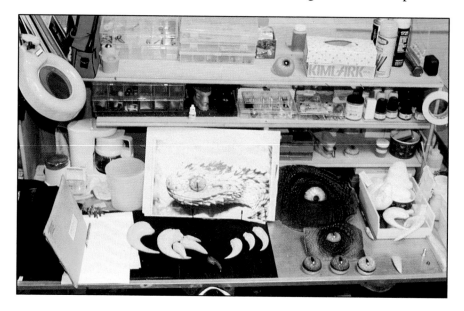

Puppet accessories, such as eyeballs, teeth and claws, were fashioned by Robert Henderstien.

Drawing from nature, Henderstien applies delicate vein patterns to a dinosaur eyeball.

tations to show what a walk would be like, what a run would be like, and some behavioral things—ten- or twelve-second situations that would show what the characters could do." Animator Randy Dutra, a longtime Tippett collaborator and specialist in animal movement, was placed in charge of developing realistic actions for the prehistoric performers. His resulting footage was compiled into a "Dinosaur Bible" and later used as the basis of pantomime by the on-set dinosaur operators. "Unlike most scenes in movies which tend to be action sequences—four- or five-second cuts—we wanted to have long running pieces of film so you could really see what the animals were doing. I thought that would be a novel approach." Once Spielberg approved the move tests, they were given to Stan Winston to assist his puppeteers in rehearsing their characters.

By the time the revised Michael Crichton screenplay was completed, Steven Spielberg was totally immersed in the shooting of *Hook*. Working with him on that project was New Jersey screenwriter Malia Scotch Marmo who had been brought on at Dustin Hoffman's behest to beef up his underwritten role. She and Spielberg promptly struck a sound rapport, and before long she found herself reworking the original Jim V. Hart script throughout.

Scotch Marmo was sitting on the set one day reading the *Jurassic Park* novel when Kathy Kennedy mentioned to her that Amblin would be making the film. "I said, 'Well, who's writing it?' And she said, 'Why, would you want to do it?' And I said, 'Yes, I'd love to do it.' That was it.

It was a very casual conversation." Casual or not, the invitation was implicit, and Scotch Marmo gradually began shifting her focus from Neverland to Jurassic Park. "Steven and I had a lot of creative contact during the filming of *Hook*. I was either there on the set or I would be on the phone with him as he went into work or whenever he left the set. And I would be faxing in script changes almost daily. So we talked a lot. But as time went on, *Hook* was occupying less and less of our conversation and *Jurassic* was occupying more and more." Once her commitment to *Hook* was completed, Scotch Marmo transitioned wholly into *Jurassic Park*.

Rather than attempt a rewrite of the Michael Crichton script, she elected to begin afresh with the novel as her basis. "I spent about a week reading everything. I read the first script, and I read the novel again and again. And I looked at all the storyboards and production art, which was quite extensive at that point. Steven generates a great deal of thought on subjects and he has storyboard artists on hand. As he thinks, they draw. Some of those drawings actually go into the film, but a lot of them are there to look at, for Steven to think about and decide if he wants them or not." Scotch Marmo also consulted with Crichton during this period. And at her request, Spielberg provided her with a copy of the book he had marked with favorite passages and annotations.

"I think the structure of Michael's script was pretty close to the final movie. It was, after all, the structure of the book. The only differences were the streamlining that one writer might do as opposed to another. Michael had done a brilliant job of presenting the science of biotechnology and raising questions about its harmlessness and the whole issue of science for profit. And he had made us believe the dinosaurs by first making us believe the science. So I knew there had to be a lot of that in there. Beyond that, I felt my job was to build up the characters, to give them more life and more purpose in the screenplay."

Though both the novel and the original screenplay were lean on characterization, Crichton was unabashed in his belief that too much emphasis on human drama might detract from the essential marvel of the story. "A lot of my work has to do with ideas of verisimilitude, of encouraging readers to believe what isn't true. If you have that focus as a writer, then to write about dinosaurs in a modern-day setting is very difficult, because it is inherently unbelievable. You're fighting disbelief every sentence of the way. So it's a tremendous psychological campaign to do a book that will cause an otherwise rational adult to buy your

In the tense finale, rampaging raptors seek human prey in the visitor center rotunda. A rendering by Craig Mullins featured tiger-like stripes on the predators, an early concept subsequently discarded.

premise for the few hours it will take to read it. No one's going to believe that there are dinosaurs, really, so it can only be kind of an enjoyable suspension of disbelief. Without that, it doesn't matter what your message is or who your characters are—nothing matters because people won't believe it. So the first thing was to make compelling dinosaurs, and that had a lot to do with how they were conceived and how they behaved and how they were introduced and talked about. That was my overriding concern."

Commencing work on the script in October 1991, Scotch Marmo labored for five months on her draft in an uncommonly close collaborative effort with Spielberg. "Usually writers get an assignment, go home, write it and turn it in. We didn't work that way. I had feedback from Steven all the time. In fact, I would send him my first fifteen pages and he would react to them. Then I'd rewrite them a little in accordance with his wishes and send them back with the next fifteen pages, so he would have thirty. And that was pretty much the process for the whole five-month period."

One of Scotch Marmo's principal changes was the elimination of the Ian Malcolm character. "I tried to incorporate a lot of Malcolm into Grant, who was kind of underdeveloped. I wanted Grant to be completely opposed to the commercialization of science—which is a big biotechnology issue. And I felt we needed to find something with Ellie and Grant and the children that made sense, so at the end of this incredible journey there was something about the experience that made them different from when they went in." Beyond that, she tried to develop cinematic means of underscoring some of Crichton's major themes. "I wanted to show the fatal flaw in trying to control nature. And I did that by juxtaposing a lot of jungle imagery with the pristine control room—things like having one wall of the visitor center uncompleted so that greenery is pushing in and vines are swinging down. Small things like windows being opened and vegetation bursting inside and little lizards that run across the sidewalk. The idea was that nature was always in the way, always pushing hard against the intrusion."

It was not until *Hook* and *Death Becomes Her* were essentially completed that energies were fully redirected into *Jurassic Park*. "We had some rough set designs that were pretty much finished," said Rick Carter, "but it wasn't until January 1992 that we really began locking into things and getting ready to build sets. It was an unusually long preparation period, but it was really helpful. If we had tried to do this picture in a normal fashion and on a normal schedule, we would have been totally out of control. As it was, a lot of storyboarding had gone on, but there was constant revising of the storyboards and the concepts for the scenes. We would show our set models to Steven and he would start doing his drawings. He does these great little drawings, very simple, but they convey what he wants to see through the lens. Then we would translate those and get them to the people who needed to see them. So it was not immaculate conception the first time out—there was a lot of fine-tuning. There would be an idea and it would go through a lot of different writers and storyboard artists and dinosaur designers—and then it

An early Tom Cranham sketch of the Jurassic Park hatchery where genetically engineered dinosaurs are introduced into the world. It was never used.

would just go by the wayside. Then a new idea would emerge and we'd see how long that one lasted. It was like survival of the fittest."

Although much of the action would take place out of doors, it was acknowledged early on that interior stage sets would afford the most flexibility when it came to working with the full-size mechanical dinosaurs that Spielberg envisioned as the principal antagonists of his film. "With large robotic creatures," said Carter, "there are a lot of mechanisms that need to be concealed; and one of the easiest ways to do that is to run them underneath the set. Now it's possible to do that in a real location by digging holes; but it's much simpler on a stage where the sets can be built on elevated platforms. Plus when you're working on stage, you can have total control over your lighting and not have to worry about weather conditions. The problem is that building a natural setting on stage—a jungle, for instance—is pretty hard to do and have it look totally convincing." Luckily, most of the major action in *Jurassic Park* was to take place at night or in rainstorms, or both, which simplified somewhat the daunting task of making stage sets look like natural outdoor environments.

Ultimately, only two stages would be required to represent the Jurassic Park exterior. Stage 27 at Universal would be filled with dense jungle foliage and would feature a giant tree in which Grant and the children, inside one of the tour vehicles, would find themselves perched precariously after the T-rex attack. Carefully planned for maximum utilization, the set would also be reconfigured to represent other areas in the park,

JURASSIC PARK - VISITORS LODGE

Clockwise from top: Another Jim Teegarden sketch of the park's visitor center accommodations. / The exterior of the center was constructed as a facade in Hawaii, with corresponding interiors built on sound stages in Hollywood. / A small-scale art department model of one of the early visitor center concepts.

including the separate locations where security chief Robert Muldoon and computer hacker Dennis Nedry meet their grisly fates. The second indoor exterior would require a space larger than Universal had to offer and was consequently slated to be built on the massive Stage 16 at nearby Warner Brothers. There, on a fabricated dirt roadway bounded by towering electrified fences, the tyrannosaurus rex would mount a terrifying assault on two stranded tour vehicles during a torrential downpour. Five other stages at Universal would eventually be filled with interior representations of the Jurassic Park visitor center, control room and other sites.

"The park is not as finished as it is in the book," noted Carter. "The movie is probably nine months or a year earlier than when the book takes place. What we were trying to convey was that this is a process. The park is in the final stages of completion, but it is never completed. The building of the perfect dinosaur is not quite there yet, the building of the perfect park is not quite there, the building of the perfect security system is not quite there. Building the perfect *anything* is impossible—especially when one is dealing with nature. The best we can do is never really good enough because we are not God—which is one of the major themes of this movie and one that relates directly to bioengineering. Just because you *can* do something, does it mean you *should* do it?

"From a design standpoint, the stars of *Jurassic Park* are the dinosaurs. That's not to say that the characters aren't important, because they are. But on a visual level, the dinosaurs are the stars. And I think the island is very strong as a setting. So I really did not want to have the park be a lot of commercialized edifices that feel shallow and overly bright and overly energetic. Even though that is something that the park would probably evolve into if it were finished, I thought as a film it would feel shallow. This is, after all, not Disneyland. What people would go to see in Jurassic Park would be the dinosaurs in their natural habitat, not a lot of man-made stuff. For the first ten years, at least, it would probably be taken very seriously—until somebody started making sideshow freaks out of the dinosaurs. So for me, that was one of the advantages of having the park not be finished. I wasn't forced to take it to its completion as an idea in terms of what it might turn into if it really were brought all the way to the point where the park was opening. If it were opening, the tendency would be to have more and more things for the people, as opposed to the park being just a window that allows one to enter into this new world that the dinosaurs are in. I tried to make it look serious in the sense that the visitor center, for example, is like a temple for dinosaurs. The bas relief bones that are seen throughout are like hieroglyphics of the earth, sculptures from the earth that tell a story. There are some very complex things going on in the control room and the labs; but as a look, I felt it should be of one element so that the concrete sense one feels is that there is the jungle and there are the dinosaurs."

To provide the vistas that would lend verisimilitude to the interior sets, three weeks of location photography would be needed in a tropical locale akin to Crichton's island off Costa Rica. Costa Rica itself was considered briefly, but then rejected when the production schedule coincided with the region's rainy season. Puerto Rico was a serious contender. But eventually chosen was the Hawaiian island of Kauai. Spielberg was upfront about his reasons for selecting the island paradise. "I think it was my age. Had I been twenty-six instead of forty-five, I might have gone to Yucatan or the Philippines or Costa Rica—someplace really rugged. But the idea of staying in a nice Hawaiian hotel with room service and a pool

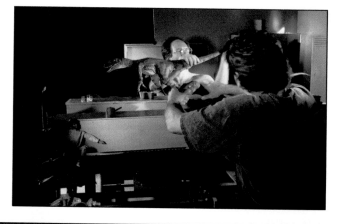

To better orchestrate his shots, Spielberg enlisted animator Phil Tippett to create a series of animatics—key action scenes choreographed and shot using small-scale models. Tippett and his team accomplished the assignment using traditional stop-motion techniques. *Top left:* Animator Tom St. Amand readies a shot of the T-rex attacking a tour vehicle. *Top right:* Crew member Kim Blanchette prepares a sequence of the raptors stalking Tim and Lex in the visitor center kitchen. *Below:* Animator Randy Dutra positions one of the raptor puppets.

for the weekend was very appealing. Fortunately, Hawaii had beautiful, lush tropical locations that were every bit as good, or better, than our other alternatives in South America or Mexico."

While the script evolved and changed, and Spielberg refined his visual set pieces, the art department kept abreast of the process with a steady stream of up-to-the-minute storyboards. Though long considered essential working tools on effects productions, storyboards provide only single-frame approximations of what a final shot might look like. Consequently, many filmmakers now employ animatics or videomatics—quickly produced effects or action scenes, shot on film or video, which can be used to determine how individual shots will intercut and to establish the overall dynamics of a sequence. Spielberg felt animatics would be useful on *Jurassic Park* and engaged Phil Tippett to provide them. "We took two major sequences in the film," said Tippett, "one with the T-rex and one with the raptors, and did quick-sketch equivalents of the scenes in full miniature using stop-motion dinosaurs and very small puppet humans. Randy Dutra began by blocking in the T-rex character with animator Tom St. Amand. Then he focused on the more complicated raptor animatics." Although the settings were sketchy and the puppets unrefined, the animation was painstakingly achieved by four effects teams over a period of four months. Each sequence was rendered in its entirety, without regard for whether individual shots would eventually be accomplished on stage or in miniature. "We blocked out Rick Carter's art-directed scenes and shot forty or fifty cuts per sequence. The idea was to make a previsualization tool to help Steven on the set and to give Stan some kind of benchmark as to what the accelerations and decelerations should be. If you can choreograph all that in advance, you are at a great advantage."

As an expedient, Stefen Dechant, working out of the art department, used an Amiga personal computer and a Video Toaster effects system to construct a three-dimensional representation of a T-rex which he then animated to generate animatics shots that were outputted onto videotape. Though essentially crude, the material was quick to produce and useful for establishing motion and pacing. Anything requiring character was left to the Tippett unit. As the stop-motion work progressed, much of the intermediate video material was replaced.

At Industrial Light and Magic, meanwhile, some vastly more sophisticated computer graphics work was underway. A year or more had

A NERVOUS REX

Crude animatics were also produced by Stefen Dechant, who utilized an Amiga personal computer and a Video Toaster effects system to model and animate rough representations of the T-rex that were useful in determining a general sense of pacing and action.

passed since Dennis Muren had had his initial discussions with Spielberg and Kennedy about *Jurassic Park*. In the intervening period, the facility had been engrossed in *Terminator 2*, producing an array of astonishing effects that would forever alter Hollywood's perception of computer graphics in the film world. Working apart from, but in consort with Stan Winston, ILM had employed computer generated imagery and advanced morphing techniques to transform actor Robert Patrick into a variety of wholly digital and puppet creations in his role as the shape-shifting liquid metal terminator in James Cameron's blockbuster film. Producers everywhere were suddenly looking at digital imagery as the new Ark of the Covenant—and *Terminator 2* went on to handily win Muren his seventh Oscar and Winston his second and third. Before long, those involved in *Jurassic Park* were contemplating a reunion of sorts for the two.

It began with a rather small-scale request. "Back before *T2*," recalled Muren, "Steven had mentioned to me that he had wanted a stampede sequence in *Jurassic Park*, with herds of animals, but he didn't know how to go about it. After our work on *T2* was finished, I picked up on that idea and thought it might be a way we could get more involved in *Jurassic Park*. At that point, Phil Tippett was going to be doing the go-motion, and we were going to be compositing his shots, getting rid of rods and doing some digital stuff. Creating herds of animals with puppets would be very difficult, so I thought maybe that was something we might be able to do with computer graphics."

Other members of the ILM computer graphics team felt they could do even more. Veteran animators Mark Dippe and Steve Williams, in fact, were already at work on a clandestine enterprise. "All of us wanted a crack at the T-rex," said Williams, "but we thought we could never get it because Stan was already in there, and so was Phil. But the attraction was strong, so I secretly started building some T-rex bones in the computer. I have a brother-in-law who lives up in Calgary, where there is one of the biggest repositories of dinosaur bones in the world, and he sent me a bunch of pamphlets and photos. We also relied on a lot of books and magazines with schematic drawings and such. I laid everything out and scanned it on a flatbed scanner and then built a skeleton from there. Then I animated a walk cycle for the rex—just the skeleton."

"There had never been much faith in computer-generated animals," observed Dippe, "at least not when we first talked about it. That was because they had never been done very well. There had been some attempts that had worked for maybe a moment or two; but they involved extreme amounts of effort, like someone spending a year of his life to get a nice four-second walking animal. But Steve and I thought we could do it, and I had been pushing Dennis for months, saying: 'Come on, tell them we can do the whole thing. Let's take a chance. We can do it.' But Dennis, being the veteran and the voice of reason that he is, kept saying: 'Maybe we can, maybe we can't. Let's see what happens.' Well, when we showed him the T-rex, his interest definitely went up a notch." Interest also went up a notch at Amblin. When Kathy Kennedy, Jerry Molen, and Lata Ryan paid a visit to ILM, they were shown the T-rex footage and responded with great enthusiasm. As a consequence, Muren was given the go-ahead to explore computer graphics as a possible means of attaining the herd shots.

One of the dinosaurs designed by the Stan Winston team, but not built, was the gallimimus, a beaked predator that looked rather like a featherless ostrich with a long tail. Working from the Winston drawings, and other sources, computer graphics artist Eric Armstrong fashioned a gallimimus skeleton in the computer and then developed an animated running cycle for it. "After we built the skeleton," said Muren, "we animated about ten of them running along in a herd. For the backgrounds, we picked some photos out of a book on Africa and scanned them into the computer. I know the kinds of shots that look neat, and I know the kinds of shots that Steven likes, so we did two angles. One was kind of looking down and over a prairie on these animals running along and the

Right: Key members of the production team: production manager Paul Deason, art director Jim Teegarden, effects supervisor Michael Lantieri, producer Kathy Kennedy, associate producer Lata Ryan, production designer Rick Carter, associate producer Colin Wilson and assistant art director Marty Kline.

Opposite: In addition to its animatronic dinosaurs, *Jurassic Park* boasted computer generated counterparts that were among the most sophisticated digital creations ever produced. Stan Winston Studio provided the computer team at Industrial Light and Magic with fifth-scale models to aid the digital modeling process. The Winston gallimimus as sculpted by Paul Mejias.

other was a view right down at ground level as they run past. It was the same animation in both cases—so we got two shots for the price of one. All we had to do was rerender." The shots were outputted onto videotape and presented to the production team at Amblin. "Everybody went nuts. No one had ever seen anything like it. Even though the gallis were just skeletons, there was so much motion and blur that your mind was filling it in. Eric had done a great job animating and Stefen Fangmeier did the comping and the rendering, and it just came together great."

Entranced by the test results, Spielberg promptly committed to the stampede sequence he had envisioned—about a half-dozen shots—and also decided to incorporate a few grand vistas dotted with grazing animals. The walking T-rex skeleton likewise prompted further testing. Stan Winston Studio provided a casting of their fifth-scale prototype, which ILM then took to Cyberware Laboratory for scanning. The Cyberware scanner, used frequently by ILM on past projects, focuses a revolving laser beam on objects or persons and records topographical data thus obtained in its computer. Designed originally to produce Styrofoam sculptures on a computerized lathe, the system has proven useful to ILM in that its data can be fed directly into their computers to create accurate three-dimensional models in digital space. Since the scanner was unable to accommodate the full six-foot-long casting, the T-rex was sliced into individual sections, scanned and reassembled in the ILM computers.

Much work was still required to refine the data and shape the dinosaur over the existing skeleton. Various computer programs were employed to attach the individual segments and cover them with a skin that had proper coloration and shading. Other programs were used to animate the completed figure. "For the background of our test shot," said Muren, "we used a still photo of some rolling hills not too far from the facility. The idea was to lay the animal into this, in broad daylight, just to see what we could really do. We did that and we scanned it out onto film. The previous tests had been on video, but we needed to see how it would work on film. The shot started out with the T-rex maybe a hundred feet away, about two-thirds the size of the frame. Then it just walked toward camera, step by step, and we sort of tilted up at the head as it passed by. Everybody went absolutely crazy. It was like nothing anyone had seen before."

On hand for the unveiling were Steven Spielberg and his producers, Dennis Muren and his ILM contingent, and Phil Tippett. "My intention had always been to use full-size dinosaurs as much as I could," stated Spielberg, "but I knew that my long shots or wide-angle shots would need to be done with stop-motion or go-motion, just like Willis O'Brien and Ray Harryhausen had done. None of us expected that ILM would make the next quantum leap in computer graphics—at least not in time for this picture. We had seen the gallimimus tests—and they were excit-

ing—but they were just skeletons and they were on video. The T-rex was complete and on film and walking in daylight, making full contact with the ground. It was a living, breathing dinosaur, more real than anything Harryhausen or Phil Tippett had ever done in their careers. At the showing, Phil groaned and pretty much declared himself extinct."

Convinced that computer graphics held the potential for producing the level of realism he had hoped to achieve with his dinosaurs, Spielberg promptly decided to scrap the go-motion work altogether and redirect his budget into the ILM digital effort. Before long, the computer graphics team unveiled an impressive new test shot—of the tyrannosaurus rex chasing a herd of fully rendered gallimimuses through a grassy clearing—that served to relieve resoundingly any latent anxiety still lingering over the advisability of committing wholeheartedly to the approach.

Tippett, who had already selected a crew of thirty and was gearing up for the massive go-motion assignment, was understandably devastated by the turn of events. "It was never our intention to ace Phil out of a job," Muren insisted. "Our stuff looked great, but we never imagined it would turn into such a big deal. We always figured that Stan would have the full-size dinosaurs and that Phil would do the go-motion puppet material and that we would have the herd footage and maybe a few T-rex shots. All these different areas of effects work would be in one movie. But Steven realized that there was something extraordinary going on here and he decided rather unexpectedly to do everything except the live stuff with computer graphics."

Tippett was prepared to bow out gracefully, but neither Muren nor Spielberg wanted to lose the expertise the veteran animator had acquired in nearly three decades of articulating rubber animals in front of stop-motion cameras. "Phil and his guys have a tremendous wealth of experience and knowledge," said Muren, "and I thought it was important that we keep Phil involved in the project to provide direction and guidance to our animators, many of whom did not really understand what a performance was. You have to remember that this is the first generation of computer animators, and they are struggling with hardware and software limitations that make the process excruciatingly painful and slow. Some of them had experience in computer character animation; but *Jurassic Park* would require photo-real animation, and very few people are as good at that as Phil is. It took some convincing, because Phil did not feel at all comfortable with computers, but I managed to persuade him that his talents were indispensable."

While Tippett struggled to learn the rudiments of digital imaging, he instituted a series of training sessions for the computer animators that was far afield from anything they had hitherto encountered. "One of the ways I direct animators is through pantomime," explained Tippett, "which helps them to cut through a lot of needless hard work by first blocking out all the shots using their own bodies. There was about a month where we had classes every day. We brought in a very talented performer named Leonard Pitt who has studied mime and Balinese dance and who was friends with Stan Laurel. He was really quite educated in how the human body moves. So the classes with him were intended to break the cycle that some people have of not wanting to use their bodies and just wanting to talk through shots or be cerebral. That was very important to me, that we be able to communicate on a direct level. Simultaneously, the animators and I would get together to critique their work on the characters that were built at the time, which were the rex and the gallimimus. We spent about a month learning how to communicate with each other, and they started coming up with some really good work."

When the final assignments were made, ILM would have fifty computer graphics shots to complete, including some of the enormous brachiosaurus and even a few raptor shots.

When her final draft screenplay was completed in March—having been rewritten as it went along—Malia Scotch Marmo submitted it to Spielberg and awaited his pronouncement upon it. "Steven is a gentleman and a friend, and we are very frank with each other. After he had analyzed the entire script, he simply said, 'I've read it twice and I think it's a miss.' As a writer, that's a terrible feeling. The natural urge is to say:

"WHICH ONE ATE YOUR HUSBAND, MA 'AM ?..."

'Give me another week. I can work it out. I know I can.' But the truth is, sometimes you do hit and sometimes you miss. It's just a shame that it takes so long to find out. So I swallowed hard and said to him something like: 'I'm really disappointed to hear that, Steven. It's your project and you have to go on. Believe me, I will mend within a day.' And I did."

With precious little time left to come up with a suitable shooting script, Spielberg immediately began casting about for another writer who could deliver on short notice. He found one in David Koepp. Having just finished work on *Death Becomes Her*—including a rewrite of the ending for a last-minute reshoot—Koepp was totally unprepared for the invitation to consider adding his name to the growing list of writers on *Jurassic Park*. He had not even read the book. Koepp promptly obtained a copy and raced through it with enthusiasm. "With an adaptation or a rewrite or anything like that, I know I can do it if my mind sort of swims immediately with the possibilities upon hearing the idea or reading the book. If nothing happens, it's pretty foolish to take the job. Fortunately, my mind swam on this one." A meeting followed with Spielberg. "Our first session was very general. Mostly we talked about the book. It was: 'So, how do you feel about dinosaurs? What in the book really overwhelmed you?' We talked about things that we loved, things that worked, characters that did and characters that didn't, things we felt *had* to be in the movie. Steven had some wonderful ideas for action scenes. The whole meeting was very exciting."

Spielberg promptly put any uneasiness Koepp may have had to rest. "Usually I don't like to do rewrites. For me, it's very hard to get into the mind of somebody else and try to follow what they were doing. But in this case, I was told I could start over—which was not a reflection on the work that the other two writers had done, but really a way to make it easier for me. If you have the world as your canvas, it really lets your own ideas run free." Electing not to read the Crichton and Scotch Marmo scripts until he had finished his own first draft, Koepp immersed himself totally in the novel, reading it a second, third, and fourth time before sitting down to write. "The toughest part of any adaptation is finding the structure. You can refine the scenes and rewrite them and make the dialogue work, but finding the spine is really hard. Like any book, a lot of *Jurassic Park* took place in people's heads; and it had a lot of plotlines that were very complicated and snarled. But, fortunately, it was written more or less like a movie, so it was not as daunting as some of the books I've adapted. Still, it was a challenge because the author of the book has 400

RIOTUS RAPTORIS

At the Winston facility, crew members Marilyn Chaney and Karen Mason detail one of the raptor suits. The suits were employed most extensively in the kitchen encounter and in the finale in which the raptors pursue the park's few remaining human survivors through the visitor center air duct system.

single-spaced pages and the screenwriter has 120 double-spaced. So they're really different animals."

Two of the centerpiece action sequences were already locked in—the tyrannosaurus rex attack on the tour vehicles and the stalking of Tim and Lex by a pair of velociraptors in the visitor center kitchen. Beyond those, Koepp had a fair amount of liberty to pursue his own choices. In paring the book down to its cinematic essence, Koepp wound up departing from earlier approaches in a number of significant ways. In the book and both completed screenplays, one of the major set pieces took place after the tyrannosaurus rex attach. Fleeing on foot through the jungle, Grant and the kids come upon the river that bisects the island and discover a raft inside a maintenance shed. Trusting that the river will deliver them to safety, the three paddle their way downstream. When the T-rex spots them from the shore, it plunges into the water and starts swimming after them. Barely evading the giant predator, the raft and its riders are eventually swept over a waterfall. "I never wanted the raft sequence. It seemed to me that at certain points in the book we were being taken on sort of an obligatory tour past every dinosaur the park had to offer. My feeling was always that once the park broke down there should be total chaos. I thought the raft trip was rather redundant. So for me, it was an easy cut to make, especially since it would have been so monstrously expensive." Other sections—such as Muldoon hunting down and tranquilizing the T-rex—were harder to let go.

The most difficult aspect of the adaptation was determining how to deal with the exposition needed to explain the extraction of dinosaur DNA and the cloning of creatures that had not walked the earth for millions of years. "That was hell," Koepp allowed. "It is the miracle of Crichton's book that he presents this outlandish premise in such a well-researched and compelling way that you actually believe it could happen. There are lengthy chapters of explanation in the book that are just wonderful. But in a movie, how do you get this across? We could have had a lab tour with people shuffling from one room to another while a bunch of scientists stood up and told them what was going on—but it would have been so dull."

Eventually the idea was put forth of a theme-park-style instructional film that could be viewed from tour vehicles as the principal characters are whisked through the lab on rails. "I'd love to take credit for it, but I think it was Steven's idea. It was brilliant. We could pop in for a few seconds here and there, put up some essential bits of information, and then get out. There was no need to have beginnings and middles and ends. We could do a lot of neat stuff that would be really fun to watch—*and* it would make sense because it's all part of the amusement part environment. Once we had that idea, everything just fell into place and we were able to do in about three pages what I was afraid was going to take fifteen. At one point, Steven laughed and said, 'We can call the narrator something like "Mr. DNA."' He was joking, but I said: 'That's *exactly* what we'll call him! That's perfect.' Because they would. It was funny, but it was really getting into a pretty weird area. Here I was writing about these greedy people who are creating a fabulous theme park just so they can exploit all these dinosaurs and make silly little films and sell stupid plastic plates and things. And I'm writing it for a company that's eventually going to put this in their theme parks and make these silly little films and sell stupid plastic plates. I was really chasing my tail there for a while trying to figure out who was virtuous in this whole scenario—and eventually gave up."

As had Scotch Marmo before him, Koepp perceived a need to flesh out the book's characterizations. Several of the secondary characters were deleted or merged into others and Ian Malcolm—his pomposity now tempered with humor—was back again. It was the principal characters that needed the most work. "There was a general feeling that Grant and Ellie weren't quite interesting enough personally and that we ought to think about how this experience was going to affect them as people, not just as scientists." The personal chemistry between the characters was boosted and given additional shading by the verbal sparring the two engage in over the issue of children—Ellie likes and wants them, Grant does not. This particular aspect dovetailed nicely with the solution to another of the character problems in the book—the fact that the children seemed largely superfluous to the plot and that Lex, the younger of the two and a terrible whiner, would have afforded Grant more than ample cause to justify his negative stance.

"The kids were kind of a challenge, because we didn't want it to seem like they were there just to have kids in the movie. Steven, in particular, is vulnerable to criticism like that, because he likes to work with kids. He works with kids awfully well, so it's not entirely fair, but the perception is there nonetheless. So our challenge was to find out why these kids were essential to the movie. To do that, we found ourselves turning back to our central theme, which is that life will find a way. With Grant as our lead and his being totally unequipped to deal with kids, we could use the presence of the kids to educate him about his own life and to show him the real value of children and the optimism they bring for the future." The idea was topped off by another Spielberg suggestion that the children's ages be reversed. With Lex now the older, Koepp was able to develop an amusing subplot relating to her prepubescent crush on the decidedly unreceptive Grant.

As the August start of principal photography bore down upon the production, work was proceeding at a quickening pace across the board. Sets were under construction, both in Hollywood and Hawaii, mechanical

The graphite fiber T-rex tail under construction. The endoskeletal structure, later covered with foam latex skin, would contain all of the mechanisms needed for fluid articulation.

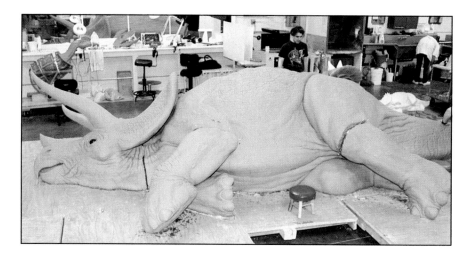

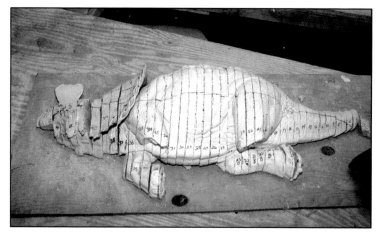

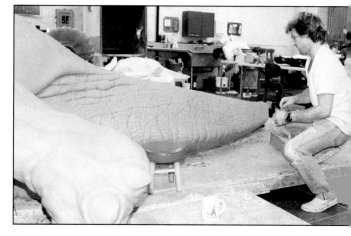

Another Winston creation was required for an early sequence of an ailing triceratops receiving treatment from the park veterinarian. *Top:* Full-scale sculpture of sick triceratops. *Above right:* Crash McCreery at work on a section of the tail. *Above left:* Like the T-rex, the triceratops was first produced in 1/5-scale, then sliced into segments that were projected up to full size to provide a sculpting form for the dinosaur. *Opposite:* Rob Ramsdel, Al Sousa, Paul Mejias and Stan Winston observe as Jon Dawe adjusts the wiring for the triceratops eye mechanism.

effects rigging was being devised and built, and computer graphics techniques were undergoing testing and refinement. Director of photography Dean Cundey—a favorite of John Carpenter and Robert Zemeckis, who had just completed his first Spielberg outing with *Hook*—was on board. So, too, was editor Michael Kahn, an Academy Award winner for *Raiders of the Lost Ark,* whose nearly unbroken collaboration with Spielberg dated back to *Close Encounters of the Third Kind.* Waiting in the wings to supply his final touch of magic was four-time Oscar-winning composer John Williams who had scored every Spielberg film, save one, since the director's feature debut with *The Sugarland Express.*

Over at the Stan Winston Studio, the sculpted T-rex had long since been sliced into pieces for mold-making and the subsequent casting of foam rubber skins. In the place it had occupied for four months during the sculpting process there now stood a formidable assemblage of welded steel and hydraulics that would serve as both skeleton and muscles for the gigantic beast. Elsewhere in the shop, the puppet raptors and spitter were nearing completion—as were the raptor suits and the closeup T-rex head that would eventually affix to a crane arm. A crane would also be used to maneuver an eight-foot-tall brachiosaur neck and head. The full creature would be seen only in computer generated form.

Sprawled on the floor was a twenty-five-foot triceratops constructed for a scene in which Grant and Ellie encounter a park veterinarian attempting to treat the ailing beast which is found lying in a field. It was the only one of the Winston creations that would make the trip to Hawaii for the location shoot. "Since the triceratops was lying on its side," said Richard Landon, "it was sculpted to be seen that way. There were fatty rolls that would not have hung properly if the animal had been stood on its feet, and the tail was flat on the underside so it would appear to have real weight to it. The most important thing Steven wanted to see was its breathing. So we hinged out the rib cage, almost right in the center of the stomach, and used a linear bearing and a drive belt crank to make it raise and lower. The head didn't need much movement, but the jaw could open and close and the tongue inside could move around. The eyes were very nice—they would open wide and do kind of a wild-eyed elephant look. The legs had a little motion, just for general life, and the tail was able to move back and forth."

Among the last major areas to be fully resolved was the cast selection. To a degree, the decisions were driven by budgetary considerations. "Basically," said Spielberg, "I wanted good, solid actors who weren't

⅕ scale sick triceratops sculpted by Joey Orosco.

Casting was not completed until shortly before the start of principal photography. *This page, from left:* Selected for the role of Tim Murphy was nine-year-old Joseph Mazello. Sam Neill was signed to portray paleontologist Alan Grant. Renowned British director Richard Attenborough returned to acting for the first time in fifteen years to play entrepreneur John Hammond. Jeff Goldblum joined on as mathematician Ian Malcolm.

Opposite page, from left: Bob Peck appeared as Jurassic Park game warden Robert Muldoon. Laura Dern was engaged to portray paleobotanist Ellie Sattler. Martin Ferrero as corporate lawyer Donald Gennaro. Ariana Richards was cast as the preteen Alexis Murphy. *Above right:* Wayne Knight essayed the role of Dennis Nedry, primary architect of the park's advanced computer systems.

going to charge outrageous prices. I didn't want to spend three to five million dollars apiece on actors for this movie. I was spending enough money on Stan Winston and Dennis Muren and Phil Tippett to make the dinosaurs, and that was where I needed the money to go. I had just done a movie-star movie with Dustin Hoffman and Robin Williams and Julia Roberts, and I had had a great time doing it, but I didn't really want to go that route on *Jurassic Park*. I wanted to go back to some of my early movies where the casting was different—with people like Richard Dreyfuss and Harrison Ford, who were still relative unknowns at the time, rather than big-time movie stars who were bringing with them the memory of their last ten hits."

At the top of Spielberg's list for the role of John Hammond was a much honored actor-turned-director who had not appeared before the cameras in fifteen years. "My first choice, without even thinking very much, was Richard Attenborough. I had tried to get him to play Tootles in *Hook*, but he was directing *Chaplin* at the time and couldn't do it. So I went back to him later, and said, 'Would you play Hammond?' I thought Michael had written it for him, whether he realized it or not. This time I was delighted that he said yes. My first choice for Ian Malcolm was always Jeff Goldblum. I went to him, and *he* said yes. So things were going well."

Filling the lead roles of Alan Grant and Ellie Sattler was not as easy. "There were a lot of possibilities for Grant and Ellie. Sam Neill was one of my original choices, but he was doing a film in Canada that overlapped our start date and I felt I couldn't wait for him. Richard Dreyfuss would have been a natural choice for me, but I knew I couldn't afford him for this picture. The same with Kurt Russell. I offered the part to Bill Hurt, but he turned it down without reading the book or the script. He said it didn't sound like the kind of movie he would be interested in making at this time in his life—and I respect that. Finally, after looking around for a couple of months, I went back to Sam Neill and wound up moving my start date about a month so I could accommodate his schedule." Spielberg's selection of Laura Dern for the role of Ellie was not an obvious one. "That was a tough choice. I never thought of Laura in the context of *Jurassic Park* because I saw her as kind of frail and always being pursued by circumstances and men. I never envisioned her as a tough gal, like Linda Hamilton or Sigourney Weaver. But, actually, she didn't need to be. She wasn't required to play that kind of character in the film. Ellie is more of a brain—a paleobotanist who loves animals and plants and is pretty much a creature of the earth. And when I got to meet Laura and spend some time with her, I found that was pretty much what she was. So it worked out nicely."

In less than ten weeks from the time he had first picked up the book, David Koepp submitted his initial draft screenplay to Steven Spielberg. Confident at last that the script was on the right track, Spielberg sent it to Malia Scotch Marmo and solicited her input. She responded with twelve pages of notes that were then forwarded to Koepp. "Malia was very helpful," said Koepp. "She made a lot of specific comments that, almost without exception, were very useful. And I found her very sweet. If the situation had been reversed, I don't know that I would have been the same. Writers generally hate to get rewritten, and I probably would have been more snide and snappish. The fact that she wasn't at all is a real credit to her." Working closely with Spielberg, and with continued input from Scotch Marmo, Koepp continued rewriting and fine-tuning his script until just before the production left for Hawaii.

Some of the eleventh-hour changes affected work that had been going on elsewhere for months, most notably the elimination of a scene in which Lex was to ride a baby triceratops. Various versions of the prehistoric infant had been in development at Stan Winston Studio; and the principal mount, a fully mechanical creation, was only days away from being completed. "Originally we were going to do a full running baby triceratops," said project coordinator Shannon Shea. "Stan had been hired years ago to make a fake boar for a movie. The whole sequence was eventually scrapped; but as a result of it, we had this big chain-driven mechanical boar that could gallop. We planned to use the same approach for the baby triceratops. Before we got too far, however, we were told that the producers were very pleased with how the computer graphics tests were coming, and they thought most of the running could be done with

Alexis rides atop a baby dinosaur in a painting by David Negron. Although the Winston team had spent months developing a mechanized baby triceratops, the idyllic sequence was cut shortly before cameras rolled.

Top left: Rods extending from the baby triceratops' feet were to be operated from below to produce the required range of movements. Using a small-scale prototype, Alan Scott and Richard Landon demonstrate the articulation approach for Stan Winston, Gerald Molen and Donna Smith. *Bottom left:* Project supervisor Shannon Shea oversaw construction of the five-foot-long infant. *Below:* Shea and Paul Mejias sculpt the baby triceratops as Stan Winston observes.

that and a mechanical rig with just a back section on it that Michael Lantieri was building. What they now wanted from us was a standing model that was full articulated, but did not have to walk or run."

While Shea supervised a team of seven sculptors in fashioning the five-foot-long baby triceratops in clay, mechanical technician Alan Scott developed an articulation plan to bring the creature to life. "Basically it was planted on the ground," said Shea, "but with rods extending out from the feet so that puppeteers underneath the stage could shift the baby's weight from foot to foot. Alan did a great job. With a little rehearsal, we all agreed it could have taken a step forward—which is

A David Negron concept for the visitor center rotunda.

more of a feat than it might seem. All the other articulations were either cable-controlled—with cables running up through the feet also—or radio-controlled. It had full motion in all of its legs, full tail motion, head and neck turning and twisting, and facial movements for the eyes, lips, tongue, and nostrils. We finished the sculpture, made the molds and skins, and assembled all the mechanics. We worked on it for more than a year and were literally two weeks away from being totally done with it when the whole sequence was cut."

The deletion of the baby triceratops was motivated by running time and logic. "Late in the writing," said Koepp, "Steven was very concerned with narrowing the focus of the script and tightening it down to two hours. We were always looking for cuts. So the triceratops ride was vulnerable from that perspective. But we also had a problem with where to put it. If we put the ride before the T-rex attack, it slowed down the movie; if we put it after the T-rex attack, why would this kid who had been attacked by this giant lizard go and ride one? Eventually we just cut it. It had been there, not because we wanted to be cute, but because we didn't want this to be just another slasher movie where the slasher happened to be a dinosaur. We wanted the animals to be really innocent. Even the meat-eaters are just out eating meat—that's what they do. We didn't want to make them bad guys. So it was important to us that the people in the movie react with a real sense of awe and wonder to what they are seeing and experiencing. Some of what we were trying to do with the baby triceratops scenes still comes across in the scene where the kids are feeding the brachiosaurus from the tree—and in the scene at night where all the dinosaur heads are hooting at each other. We wanted to include a lot of that kind of stuff. I just hope it comes off as lyrical as it sounded when we wrote it."

In the end, all parties were pleased with the progression from novel to screenplay—even Michael Crichton. "The script was changed and refined a *lot* after my draft—in ways that I think are really very good, I should add. As a writer, I think there are two kinds of changes that other people can make. There are the changes that I look at and I feel that I might have actually made myself—so I'm not troubled by those. Then there are the other changes, even very minor ones that one would think are not important, that just seem totally alien to what I would do. They really throw me off completely. The feeling that I have about the *Jurassic Park* script is that it all seems very compatible with my way of thinking— it fits in my mind. So I read through it, I'm sure, imagining that I wrote much more of it than I actually did."

"When Michael and I went into this," Spielberg remarked, "I told him: 'By the way, don't expect me to be shooting this in eight months. This is at least a two-year prep. We have a lot of mechanical and visual effects to work out.' Frankly, I thought I was giving him an exaggerated preproduction time. I wanted to give myself a little room to be wrong. But as it turned out, I didn't know how right I was. From the time we officially went into preproduction to the first day of shooting, it was exactly two years and one month, to the day."

PART TWO

PRODUCTION

On Monday, August 24, 1992, the cast and crew of *Jurassic Park* gathered at Olekele Canyon on the island of Kauai for the first three-week leg of what was scheduled to be an eighty-two-day shoot. Remotely located near the area documented as the wettest spot in the United States, the canyon greeted the production company with an intermittent drizzle of rain. More an irritation than a hindrance, the rain nonetheless served as a subtle illustration of nature's unerring ability to thwart even the most carefully orchestrated of man's efforts—a central theme of the film the company had come here to make. More compelling and frightening demonstrations of that theme would follow.

Led by Steven Spielberg, it was a distinguished and dedicated corps now assembled on Kauai. Some, like producer Kathleen Kennedy, had been zealously preparing for this day for more than two years. During that time, the producer had worked with Spielberg in the collaborative style the two had developed through their long and successful association. "Steven and I had talked about every detail of the production by the time cameras rolled," Kennedy commented, "which gave me a huge advantage from a producing standpoint. By the time we got to shooting *Jurassic Park,* we knew exactly where we were going with this movie; and we knew exactly how much it was going to cost. The two years we'd spent in preparation made all the difference when we got to principal photography."

Sharing production responsibilities with Kennedy was Gerald R. Molen. "Kathy handled the creative side of things," said Molen, "while I handled more of the physical production end, working closely with the production manager, the agents and the attorneys. That arrangement proved beneficial to the production. Kathy was right there on the set

Opposite: Freed from her paddock due to a breakdown of the park's security system, the tyrannosaurus rex launches a vicious attack on a stalled tour vehicle carrying John Hammond's visiting grandchildren. *Below:* Director Steven Spielberg on location in Hawaii.

with Steven, which was a benefit to her because it made her more directly involved with the actual filming of the movie. It was also a benefit to the shooting unit because they were able to take advantage of her valuable input."

Working closely with both Kennedy and Spielberg on location was director of photography Dean Cundey. Given the lengthy preproduction phase, Cundey had come onto the project relatively late—although he had kept abreast of its progress through his informal association with production designer Rick Carter. "I would talk with Rick about what was happening on *Jurassic Park*," Cundey recalled, "more out of curiosity than anything else. It seemed like a very exciting project, and I would stop in periodically at Rick's office to look at the drawings and set models." Making the transition from casual observer to major player, Cundey was officially engaged as director of photography when preproduction finally moved into full gear.

Long before arriving in Hawaii with his camera crew and equipment, Cundey had determined the cinematic style of the film in a series of brainstorming sessions with Spielberg. Some of these sessions had the director and cinematographer studying concept paintings rendered by the art department, while others were devoted to analyzing scenes from various films that Spielberg found visually appealing. "Steven wanted a very realistic look for *Jurassic Park* so that the audience would feel as if they were actually *in* the park, as much as possible. My style tends toward a realistic, crisp, color-saturated look; so that approach suited me well."

Because most of *Jurassic Park*'s action would be shot on sound stages

Below: Director of photography Dean Cundey. Lower left: Producer Kathleen Kennedy confers with Spielberg on location. Lower right: Producer Gerald R. Molen in costume for his bit part as park veterinarian Gerry Harding.

A location scout photograph of Kauai. After considering a number of island locales, the production team chose Kauai to represent Isla Nublar, the Costa Rican setting of Jurassic Park.

in Los Angeles, Cundey's primary objective on Kauai was to capture the island's beautiful, wide vistas and thus open up the film visually. "Most of the storyboards illustrated a film that was pretty confined in its images," Cundey noted. "You can only see so far beyond the trees in a jungle. So one of the reasons for going to Kauai was to reveal this island where the story takes place. We wanted to get larger backgrounds behind some of the action—in the daytime, particularly—and Kauai had wonderful locations to show off." Although scenically spectacular, the tropical locale was not without its challenges. "Hawaii is notorious for its changing light—the clouds are constantly coming and going. So we would be working in bright sunlight one moment, and in the next we would be in soft overcast light that didn't match at all. The way around that was to have the lighting on hand to create our own sunlight, to some extent. We could never duplicate it exactly, but there were little tricks we could do with lighting and film exposures to create a match from scene to scene."

Other members of the first unit present in Hawaii were lead actors Sam Neill, Richard Attenborough, Laura Dern and Jeff Goldblum.

While the design and technical aspects of production had been in progress for months, even years, casting of the key roles of Alan Grant, John Hammond, Ellie Sattler and Ian Malcolm had not been completed until late in preproduction. As a consequence, the actors had been afforded only a brief few weeks to prepare for their respective roles before filming commenced.

Richard Attenborough's situation was particularly thorny since the renowned British director was in postproduction for his own film, *Chaplin,* at the time cameras rolled on *Jurassic Park.* In a career that had spanned half a century, Attenborough had starred in more than fifty films, among them such classics as *The Great Escape* and *The Sand Pebbles,* making his directorial debut in 1969 with *Oh! What a Lovely War.* In the years since, he had gone on to direct a number of epic-scale films, including *A Bridge Too Far, Cry Freedom* and *Gandhi,* the latter earning him an Academy Award for best director. After a fifteen-year hiatus from acting, Attenborough had accepted the Hammond role primarily because of Spielberg's willingness to accommodate his postproduction responsibilities. "Steven said he understood that I was finishing up *Chaplin,*" Attenborough related, "and that I had commitments there, but that they would schedule around them. And I told him that, under those conditions, I would give my right arm to do *Jurassic Park.* In the past few years I've had quite a number of roles offered to me, but no one has ever said. 'We'll work around your commitments.'"

It was not only the flexible scheduling, but also the flamboyant role itself that had seduced Attenborough. As drawn in the script, John Hammond is a complex character with an appealing, childlike enthusi-

Above: Cast members Jeff Goldblum, Richard Attenborough, Laura Dern, Martin Ferrero and Sam Neill gather for a read-through of the script early in the three-week Kauai shoot.
Below: Richard Attenborough as Jurassic Park visionary John Hammond.

asm that is tainted by a dangerous propensity to play God. "I thought the part was fascinating, and quite different from the Hammond in the book," Attenborough observed. "In the book, Hammond really was a bit of a sod—even villainous to a certain point. The screenplay illustrated a man of some ruthlessness and determination, but also considerable charm, who uses that charm and a kind of impresario flair to persuade people."

Despite the complexity of the role and his many outside obligations, the seventy-year-old Attenborough was to make a relatively painless transition from directing back into acting. "Actors are like circus horses in a way—all we've got to do is get the smell of the sawdust, and our hooves start and off we go. But I must say, the pure physical work of learning lines was something I had fallen out of the habit of doing. In some ways, acting is much tougher work than directing. You not only have to remember lines, you also have to concentrate and bring everything into focus at the moment. The experience was a real joy—working with Steven and an enchanting cast who treated me as a sort of aging, benevolent uncle—but, even so, directing remains my first love."

Like Attenborough, Sam Neill had also been required to change gears quickly from one project to the next. He had, in fact, returned from Toronto where he had just completed *Family Pictures* with Anjelica Huston on a Thursday, and by the following Monday was in Hawaii to begin production on *Jurassic Park*. Much in demand in recent years, Neill was accustomed to back-to-back projects. Raised in New Zealand, the actor had first distinguished himself in Australian films, such as *My Brilliant Career*, before appearing on the American scene with *The Final Conflict*, the last entry in the *Omen* trilogy. Subsequent projects included *A Cry in the Dark, Dead Calm* and *The Hunt for Red October*.

During infrequent breaks in his hectic schedule, Neill had prepared his role as Alan Grant, the renowned scientist whose lifelong dream to walk among real, living dinosaurs becomes a nightmare in Jurassic Park. "I read the book," said Neill, "and I spoke with paleontologist Jack Horner for a bit. I also came up with a personal history of Grant—something just to help me, which may or may not have coincided with what anybody else thought about the character. Steven had decided that Grant didn't have to be American, that perhaps he was from Australia and had lived here a long time. I saw him as someone who had graduated from an American university and had stayed in America his entire career. And by being unorthodox and a radical and a groundbreaking paleontologist, he

Sam Neill discusses an upcoming scene with Spielberg. Slated for the location shoot were daytime exteriors, including scenes of the visiting scientists' arrival and their first, awestruck sightings of the park's prehistoric wildlife.

has become something of a star, with an avid following."

Neill's first few days in Hawaii were devoted to shooting scenes with Hammond's grandchildren, Tim and Alexis, played by Joseph Mazello and Ariana Richards. One of the film's humorous ironies is that it is Grant—whose disdain for children is revealed early on—who becomes the children's protector and near-constant companion. The scientist's disinterest in kids—a major point of contention in his relationship with Ellie—is sorely tested by Tim's incessant questions and Lex's pubescent crush as the story unfolds. "It's not that Grant dislikes children particularly," Neill noted, "it's just that he is too caught up in his professional life to have time or energy for them. They are a kind of a foreign species to him, so they make him anxious." Since the majority of his scenes would involve interaction with Mazello and Richards, it was fortunate that Neill, the father of three, did not share Grant's aversion to youngsters. "I didn't really think of them as children; I thought of them as actors. They were both extraordinarily talented, and we got on well. I happen to actively like children anyway, so it wasn't a problem for me."

One of the more inspired changes from the book to the film, in terms of character development, had been the reversing of the children's ages. In Crichton's book, Lex had been the younger sibling, a tomboy with an irritating tendency towards whining. In contrast, Tim had been the big brother whose nose was always in a book. For the film, Spielberg chose to make Tim the younger sibling, with Lex a budding twelve-year-old— a decision prompted primarily by casting considerations. "I had met

Also scheduled for location photography were scenes featuring Grant, Tim and Lex as they attempt to make their way back to the visitor center after surviving the T-rex attack. Stopping to rest, the trio examines one of Grant's paleontological finds.

Joey Mazello when I was casting *Hook* and was looking for a boy to play Robin Williams' son. He was a little young for the part in *Hook,* but I thought he was very talented. Then when I read *Jurassic Park,* I realized he would be perfect for Tim." At nine years old, Mazello was already something of a veteran in the movie business. He had won his first leading role in the TV movie *Unspeakable Acts* at age five, and since then had appeared in *Presumed Innocent* and costarred in *Radio Flyer.*

Despite Mazello's talent and experience, however, his casting created something of a dilemma for the director. "He looked younger than his age," Spielberg said, "and I realized that if I cast Lex younger than Tim, she would look about five years old—which was much too young to put in jeopardy with these dinosaurs. It would have turned the audience against us completely. So I thought it would be best to cast older for the girl; and that turned out great because it gave me the bonus of introducing Lex's preadolescent crush on Grant."

Watching television one night, Spielberg had spotted actress Ariana Richards. The young girl had delivered a much lauded performance in the TV movie *Switched at Birth,* and had appeared in feature films such as *Tremors* and *Prancer.* "She looked like Lex to me. I had her come in to read; but I was really less interested in her line readings than I was in seeing if she could show fear. I asked Janet Hirshenson, the casting director, to have her stand in the room and scream for three minutes and show me the tape. I got the tape the next day, and I hadn't seen screams like that since Fay Wray was undone at the sacrificial altar by King Kong. I had

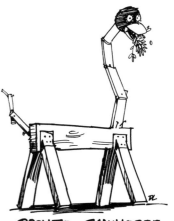

BRONTO - SAWHORSE

Ariana come in the next day—ironically, at the same time that I was interviewing Laura Dern for the first time—and I cast her right in front of Laura. Laura kind of laughed and said, 'What about me?' "

Cast shortly thereafter in the role of Ellie Sattler, Dern need not have been concerned. Nominated for an Academy Award in 1991 for her performance in *Rambling Rose,* the actress had already, at age twenty-five, earned a reputation for sensitive portrayals in challenging, character-driven films such as David Lynch's *Blue Velvet* and *Wild at Heart. Jurassic Park* was to mark a definite departure for her. "It was totally unlike anything I had ever done," Dern commented. "For one thing, it was a genre film; and while the characters were really important, they were almost secondary to the dinosaurs. The role was also a new one for me. I have been perceived in the past as a kind of woman-child. But Ellie is a strong, mature woman in a mature relationship with a man, as well as a respected paleontologist."

Like her fellow cast members, Dern had been brought onto the *Jurassic Park* project fairly late in the game. "I really only had a couple of weeks to prepare before we started shooting. I worked with some paleontologists who were kind enough to teach me as much as I could learn in such a limited amount of time. I spent a little time with Jack Horner, and I read his book. I also went to the Natural History Museum in Los Angeles, and the curators there showed me how to prepare a fossil. It all helped me to understand some of what I was talking about in the movie."

The short preparation period had, however, afforded Dern sufficient

Left: Laura Dern as Ellie Sattler, one of the paleontologists invited to inspect Jurassic Park. *Right:* Jeff Goldblum as mathematician Ian Malcolm, who employs the chaos theory to predict the downfall of the Jurassic Park experiment.

Led by Hammond, the invited scientists—accompanied by lawyer Donald Gennero—embark on their tour of Jurassic Park. For exterior shots of the visitor center, a massive facade was constructed on Kauai.

opportunity to work directly with Spielberg in fleshing out her character. "*Jurassic Park* was the kind of movie that required making the characters and relationships real through the action of the movie itself," Dern remarked. "So Steven and I had to find the spots where we could do that, without turning the movie into something it wasn't. There had to be more forethought about the characters and what was *really* important to say than would have been necessary in a character piece where the whole movie was about that. We had to plan where we could get it in, because there was so little of it." One of the character concerns that Dern addressed with Spielberg was how to make Ellie an integral part of the story, rather than just an obligatory female love interest. "Fortunately, Ellie had been written as a strong character—she saves the day more than once in the film—and I really tried to emphasize her strong qualities."

Of all the casting decisions he had had to make, none was easier for Spielberg than the selection of Jeff Goldblum. Goldblum had been the director's first choice for the role of Ian Malcolm, the brilliant mathematician whose persistent skepticism regarding the Jurassic Park experiment is ultimately validated. Goldblum had established his career with intelligent, often offbeat characterizations in films as diverse as *The Fly, The Big Chill,* and *The Adventures of Buckaroo Banzai.* "Everything about this project interested me—the dinosaurs, the people who would be making the dinosaurs, the cast," Goldblum said. "I knew it would be great. And I liked the role very much. Malcolm is kind of mysterious and seductive and sensitive. He is also skeptical and cynical—but not misguidedly so. As it turns out, he is absolutely right."

Both the cast and crew were primed and ready by the time principal photography began in the remote canyons of Kauai. Slated to be filmed were daytime exteriors of the visiting scientists' arrival at the park, as well as exteriors of the raptor pen and the maintenance shed where, later in the picture, Ellie attempts to restore the park's power system. Also scheduled were scenes in which the awestruck visitors spot their first dinosaurs—a fifty-foot brachiosaur feeding at a leafy treetop and a gallimimus herd running across a distant plain—plus a poignant scene featuring an ailing triceratops. With the excitement and jitters typical of the first day of filming, the 140-member production company began its adventure in Jurassic Park.

Weeks before the first unit's arrival on Kauai, art department and construction crews had come to the island to build a variety of sets which would represent structures inside Jurassic Park. Principal among them were the visitor center exterior—a sixty-foot-tall, nearly two-hundred-foot-long building facade—the exterior of the maintenance shed, and expanses of a massive electrified fence that, in the story, served to contain the more ferocious of the park's inhabitants. Rick Carter had overseen the design of all the sets during preproduction, ably supported by art directors Jim Teegarden and John Bell. "Generally, I would do concept drawings of the sets," explained Bell, "while Jim, who has an architectural background, would get into the details, carrying those concepts out all the way to the blueprint stage."

Under the supervision of Teegarden and construction coordinator John Villarino, set construction had begun in early June, nearly three months before the start of principal photography. To take advantage of Kauai's dramatically varied landscapes, the sets were fashioned at several different sites on the island—some so rugged and remote that they could only be accessed by off-road, four-wheel-drive vehicles. "We were spread out all over the island," noted Villarino, "and that was our biggest ordeal, just managing the logistics of it. We had to build a lot of roads in Hawaii just to get the crew in—a hundred-thousand-dollars' worth of roads, in fact. When it was time for us to leave, the locals actually thanked us."

Although logistically challenging, the contrasting locales served to surround the sets in scenic splendor. "There is a sense you get in some movies that you've really traveled somewhere," observed Rick Carter, "and *Jurassic Park* has that, largely because of Kauai and the power of its

Top: The heavily fortified raptor pen, another set built in the remote canyons of Kauai. *Center:* The visitor center facade under construction. *Bottom:* The completed visitor center facade.

imagery and diversity. There is a very romantic quality about the island, but it is not all benign. There are areas which are some of the most beautiful pasture land in the world; other areas are more mountainous, with rougher terrain. For *Jurassic Park,* we took everything Kauai had to offer and jam-packed it into our own little island."

In the film, the team of scientists commissioned by Hammond to inspect Jurassic Park—and thus secure its continued backing by nervous investors—arrives at Isla Nublar by helicopter, and is then transported to the visitor center. Exteriors of the group's arrival at the center were photographed in front of the massive facade in Hawaii, while scenes featuring the characters inside the building would be filmed later, on an interior set at Universal. As the visual centerpiece of the park, the visitor center—both interior and exterior—had been addressed very early in the preproduction design effort.

John Bell had initiated the process with a thorough examination and analysis of the Hammond character. "I kept thinking about who this John Hammond was," said Bell. "What kind of name is Hammond? Well, probably English. So I thought he might have had a reserved upbringing, maybe a religious upbringing. I thought this whole thing with the dinosaurs might have been a born-again kind of event for him, as if he was giving the dinosaurs a second chance. I started to think of rebirth, and came up with this egg shape which is seen throughout the movie. The main door of the visitor center has a big amber egg on it, with lines radiating off of it. The shape of the building itself was loosely based on a temple in Jerusalem that had influenced Rick; so the religious influ-

Left: Tim Murphy scales the deactivated electrified fence surrounding the park.
Right: Long expanses of the twenty-four-foot-tall fence were erected on location, a formidable task relegated to special effects supervisor Michael Lantieri.

ence was there, as well. The circle was another strong design element—Rick liked it as a symbol of something that is never-ending."

Although more straightforward in terms of design, the huge scale of the electrified fence—featured primarily in shots of the tour vehicles driving past the tyrannosaurus rex paddock—presented the crew with one of its most difficult construction projects. "It was an amazing thing to see on location," observed Carter. "It was twenty-four feet tall—bigger than any fence you would *ever* see in the real world, because we have no reason to build a fence that high. Once you're over twelve feet, what are you keeping out? The mere scale of it made it really scary, because you know something *big* must be behind it."

John Bell had conceptualized the formidable structure as huge steel I-beams protruding from a series of thick concrete towers, with heavy cable spanning the forty-foot distances in between. Because of the difficulty of securing such long lengths of cable, however, the spacing between towers was eventually shortened to thirty feet, with additional vertical dividers placed at fifteen-foot intervals. Angled back dramatically, and equipped with blinking, cold blue lights at the top, the fence was intended to convey a dramatic sense of foreboding.

The special effects crew was tasked with erecting the massive fences at the Kauai location—a challenging prospect given the ruggedness of the terrain. "One of our locations in Hawaii was a canyon that was a forty-five-minute, four-wheel drive to get into," Michael Lantieri explained. "So we had to haul all of this steel up there, drill holes like you would for telephone poles, pour concrete, and then pull all of the cables, which were three-quarter-inch aluminum with steel in the middle. We used more than six miles of that cable—it was like running power from the Hoover Dam to Los Angeles."

For extended shots of the tour vehicles tracking alongside the barrier, long stretches of the fence had to be erected. "Our longest expanse consisted of eight of the big towers," said Lantieri, "with thirty feet of cable in between each of them. It was really a headache to get the cable taut, but Steven kept emphasizing that he didn't want the cable to sag—he wanted it to look tight. We found a company over there that had experience setting power lines through the mountains in Kauai; and we hired two of their guys and a truck to help us out. It was an enormous job—and for very little payoff. People will look at the movie and say, 'Oh, there's a fence,' never realizing what it took to get it there. It was hard on my crew. About the third week into it, they started saying: 'You know, we

Sam Neill, Joseph Mazello and Ariana Richards position themselves on the fence structure in preparation for a shot.

jumped at the chance to go to Hawaii—when do we see the beach? All we've seen so far is rain, mosquitos and heavy jungle.' "

However daunting, erecting the fence in Kauai had been a fairly straightforward construction assignment. Michael Lantieri would also be responsible for a variety of physical effects executed on location. A number of shots revealing the tour vehicles traveling through the park were among those that required Lantieri's special skills. As designed by John Bell, the vehicles themselves were modified Ford Explorers that featured large, bubble-shaped roofs made of plexiglass, and a colorful, customized paint job complete with the Jurassic Park logo. To simulate the tour car being propelled on rails in typical amusement park fashion, Lantieri had laid down track—for cosmetic purposes only—and devised a "blind drive" system. "We rigged the car so that we could remote-control the steering, acceleration and brakes. Someone would lay down in the luggage section with the remote control and a hidden monitor, and drive the car that way."

Lantieri also rigged interactive effects for scenes involving computer generated dinosaurs, working in tandem with a crew from Industrial Light and Magic who were on hand in Hawaii to oversee the filming of plates that would provide backgrounds for their computer animation. Among the computer generated dinosaur elements that would be produced by ILM were a fifty-foot-tall brachiosaur and an entire herd of gallimimus. While showing his guests the grounds shortly after their arrival at the park, John Hammond is delighted to mark their astonished reactions to the sight of the brachiosaur grazing at a nearby tree. In a later scene, the visitors spot a gallimimus herd running across a plain, then dash for cover as the herd suddenly changes direction and begins to charge up a hill toward them.

Because the gallimimus herd was to be realized solely through computer animation that would not be added until much later, the background plate of the plain photographed in Hawaii would be devoid of any physical evidence of the animals. Employing techniques similar to those they had used on *Who Framed Roger Rabbit,* Lantieri's crew was tasked with providing the interaction of the herd on the vacant plain. "There were a number of CG shots in the film where, in the initial plate, there was nothing at all," Lantieri explained. "So we would make an effect happen, and then ILM would time their computer generated dinosaur so that it looked as if the animal had made it happen. For the gallimimus sequence, there were supposed to be shots of the animals jumping over logs as they ran. So we designed a log that would bounce a little bit, with chunks of bark flying off as if an animal's hooves had hit it."

The computer generated elements also had to be accommodated when plates for the brachiosaur sequence were photographed. Filming the sequence required fifty-foot-tall "story poles"—markers that would guide the camera operator's framing of the scene. Constructing and mounting the story pole was a task that fell to the art department. "Throughout the show," noted Marty Kline, "our biggest problem was just dealing with the size of these animals. They were huge, which meant that all the accessories had to be huge, as well. A story pole is simple enough—just a piece of wood marked off at one-foot intervals—but because the brachiosaur was supposed to be over fifty feet tall, it became an enormous job just to make a story pole for her. It had to be mounted

Top left: One of the Jurassic Park tour vehicles outside the T-rex paddock. *Top right:* Spielberg confers with Michael Lantieri, whose effects crew was responsible for rigging the vehicles with a blind-drive system to simulate theme-park-style automated tour vehicles. *Bottom:* To further the illusion, Lantieri's crew laid down miles of track on location.

on a truck and surrounded with twenty feet of steel cage just to get up to where her shoulders would be. Then there was another thirty-foot rod on top of that, with a little bar at the end to represent her head. It was a really big job."

Not all of the dinosaur scenes shot in Hawaii featured computer animated creatures. Early in their tour of the park, the visitors—no longer able to contain their excitement—escape the confines of their tour cars and head for a small stand of trees where Jurassic Park veterinarian Gerry Harding is treating a sick triceratops. Finding the animal heavily sedated and lying on her side, the scientists are afforded the opportunity to conduct a hands-on examination of the beast. Stan Winston and key members of his team had made the trek to Hawaii to shoot the scene, which utilized their full-size, mechanical triceratops. Originally, all of the mechanical dinosaurs had been slated for use within the controlled environment of a studio sound stage. Ultimately, however, Spielberg decided that the triceratops would be more effective in the real rain forest surroundings of Kauai. "All the dinosaurs that were shot on stage were in scenes that took place at night in the rain, or at dawn, or at dusk," Spielberg explained. "But the sick triceratops scene took place right in the middle of the day, and I didn't think we could naturally create that on a stage. So I asked that we spend a little bit more money to get the triceratops to Hawaii. And I think it really paid off—the animal is right there in the jungle, rather than on a small section of a stage."

The creative decision to shoot the triceratops in Hawaii, at the top of

A key scene shot in Hawaii was one in which the tour group comes upon an ailing triceratops. Steven Spielberg and Kathleen Kennedy pose with the full-size animatronic dinosaur designed and built by the Stan Winston Studio.

the shooting schedule, threw a curve ball to the Stan Winston team. Not only was the triceratops the second largest creature being built by the studio, it had also initially been scheduled for shooting near the *end* of production. For Winston, taking the sick triceratops to Hawaii meant completing the creature a full three months earlier than he had anticipated. "It was a double-edged sword," Winston admitted. "On the one hand, it seemed almost an impossibility to get this enormous dinosaur finished so quickly. Yet, this was the first dinosaur that we were really going to get a good look at in the movie, and I thought it would be wonderful to have this vista of Hawaii behind it. There was no question that *that* would be the best way to show off this animal. So I realized that, difficult or not, the sick triceratops *should* be there in Hawaii; and I decided that I would do whatever I had to do to get it there. By doing that, we would also be getting things off to a good start with Steven."

An all-out, accelerated effort was initiated to complete the mechanical triceratops in time for the Hawaii location shoot. Amidst the last-minute rush, Winston consoled himself with the fact that, in the story, the creature was supposedly ill—a story point that would act as a convenient cover if some of its articulations failed to function. "Because it was sick, it really had to do very little. If something went wrong, it would just mean the dinosaur was a little sicker. 'Oh, the foot is not working? Fine, the dinosaur is too sick to move her foot.' So there was kind of a way out there. But as it turned out, everything worked. She was beautiful, dynamic, alive—just an incredible beast. And that set the tone for the shooting of this movie—we had delivered and everyone was happy."

Clockwise from upper left: Spielberg and Dean Cundey prepare a shot of the triceratops with camera operator Ray Stella and assistant director John Kretchmer. / Stan Winston, Spielberg and operator Shannon Shea with the triceratops. / Ellie and Grant attend to the ailing creature while Tim observes. / The triceratops on location in Hawaii.

Laura Dern, whose character was particularly taken by the animal in the scene, found the presence of the creature on the set so early in the schedule to be tremendously beneficial from an acting standpoint. "I had been told by other actors who have worked in films with mechanical creatures that this was not going to be a lot of fun," Dern remarked. "And Steven had warned me about that, too. But acting with these dinosaurs was wonderful. In fact, my favorite scene was the one where I was working with the sick triceratops—she was so beautiful and real, and I was truly moved, as I am in the scene, just by being with her. That creature actually helped me act in the scene and made me fall in love with her. It was a beautiful experience."

Friday, September 11, was slated to be the company's last day on Kauai. The shoot had gone remarkably well, and all that remained to be filmed were background plates for the gallimimus stampede. But suddenly, the happily uneventful shoot *became* eventful with the devastating arrival of Hurricane Iniki. Determined to be the worst storm to hit the islands in this century, Iniki tore through Kauai with sustained winds up to 165 miles per hour and gusts as high as 180 miles per hour. Spielberg's first warning of the storm came at three-thirty on that Friday morning when he was awakened by the sound of chairs being folded up and removed from the beach area of his hotel. "I went to my balcony and saw the staff with flashlights, running the chairs off the beach. I knew something was wrong, so I turned on the news and found out that Iniki was making a beeline for Oahu and Kauai. I had my assistant awaken everyone on the production team so that we could try to figure out a way to get us all off the island before it hit. But by dawn it was clear that the airport was closed and no flights were being allowed in by the FAA. We had called for our private charter jet, but it had been directed to land on the big island and to stay far away from Kauai. So we knew at that point that we were in the hands of the American Red Cross, the hotel staff and civil defense."

By eleven o'clock that morning, the entire company had been sequestered in the hotel ballroom to nervously wait out the storm. "I kept remembering the John Ford film *Hurricane,* where all the people took refuge in a church, and waves were pounding against adobe walls and Polynesians were drowning—and I wondered if that was going to happen to all one hundred forty members of our cast and crew. These thoughts were going through everybody's minds—how bad was this going to be? They were predicting that it would be a Force five hurricane, which was one level worse than Hurricane Andrew—and we had all seen what Andrew had done to Florida." By three o'clock that afternoon, the hotel had lost all power. "It was pretty hellish for the next couple of hours until the eye passed over us. We lost our roof; but our ceiling held, even though it was pouring water. Finally, seven-and-a-half hours after we'd taken shelter, we were allowed to go back to our rooms." It was not until the following morning that Spielberg was able to witness the aftermath of the storm. "Iniki had gone through Kauai like the big bad wolf at the house made of straw. Every single structure was in shambles; roofs and walls were torn away; telephone poles and trees were down as far as the eye could see. It was the worst devastation I had ever personally witnessed."

Of primary concern to the production team was finding a way to get the company off the island as quickly as possible. With all the roads out of the hotel impassable by car or truck, producer Kathy Kennedy ran the five miles to the airport early in the morning after the storm. "I got to the airport and there was no one there," Kennedy recalled, "except for two people who were driving up and down the runway checking for damage. It was clear that the control tower was destroyed. I met the people who ran the airport and explained that we had a film crew stuck at the hotel. But I understood that we were not a priority—getting a movie crew off the island was not something they were terribly worried about at that point."

Having assessed the airport situation, Kennedy ran back to the hotel to brief the company. "By that time, our crew had helped in getting some of the roads cleared. They had also been able to hook up the electricity because we had our own generators. Four of us went back to the airport in a little jeep. When we got there, we saw that they had set up a makeshift tower, and some military planes and a little Piper Cub carrying some Salvation Army people had landed. I arranged to hitch a ride with the Piper Cub pilot when he flew back to Honolulu so I could try to track down the studio jet we'd called before the storm hit. When I got to Honolulu, I found the jet—but I still didn't know how we were going to get it into Kauai, because the airport there was still restricted to military transport only."

While attempting to make arrangements with Hawaiian Airlines, Kennedy found help from a surprising source. "A guy came up to me and said, 'Do you know who I am?' And I said, 'No.' And he said, 'Does the line, "That's my pet snake Reggie," mean anything to you?' It was the pilot from *Raiders of the Lost Ark*! I couldn't believe it. He had been flying a DC-3 in and out of Kauai, loaded with medical personnel and supplies. So he and I worked out a plan with the National Guard—we would fly to Kauai with doctors and nurses on the studio jet and with medical supplies on a Hawaiian Airlines DC-8, and we'd get the crew out on those jets. And that's what we did. Everybody was out within forty-eight hours after the storm, and we lost only one day of shooting." Two weeks later, the production would send a film crew to Oahu to pick up the last day's shooting lost to Iniki. "Kauai was just ravaged, so we had to do all new location scouts. Even shooting aerials of Kauai was impossible because most of the trees were either down or stripped of all their leaves."

Despite the unscheduled appearance of Hurricane Iniki, the Hawaii

Top left: Near the end of the location shoot, Hurricane Iniki devastated the island of Kauai and brought a temporary halt to production. *Bottom left:* Members of the film crew help to clear the roads surrounding their hotel on the morning after the storm. *Above:* The terrifying Iniki experience was captured on T-shirts designed by David Lowery and distributed to the cast and crew.

shoot had been a resounding success. "We brought in the first three weeks of shooting pretty much on budget and on schedule," noted Spielberg, "except for the day we lost to Iniki, which the insurance company paid for. And we hardly missed a step—we got off the island on a Sunday, and by the following Tuesday we were shooting on the lot at Universal."

Except for a brief foray to the Mojave Desert, the remainder of the first unit photography would take place on sound stages at Universal Studios and Warner Brothers. Among the first stage sets to be utilized was the kitchen interior on Universal's Stage 24, the setting for a major sequence in which Tim and Lex are stalked by two raptors. In the story, Grant has taken the children to the deserted visitor center for safety, unaware that the raptors, the most cunning and fierce of the Jurassic Park predators, have escaped from their pen and are now on the loose inside the building. After Grant departs, Tim and Lex detect the raptors in the dining room and quickly take refuge in the center's spacious kitchen, soon followed by the wily beasts. In a terrifying game of cat-and-mouse, the kids finally make their escape when one animal is disabled and the other is trapped inside a giant walk-in freezer.

Spielberg had envisioned the sequence as one of the film's most frightening. "The raptors are very intelligent and cooperative in their planned attack—and that in itself is scary. I kept telling myself to imagine I was not making a dinosaur movie, but rather a movie about four Bengal

Losing only one day to Iniki, the production returned to Universal Studios to film the sequence in which Tim and Lex are pursued by a pair of velociraptors in the visitor center kitchen. *Top left:* Tim tries to hide from raptor in freezer. *Top right:* The industrial-size kitchen, as designed by John Berger. *Below:* After spotting the crafty predators in the dining room, Tim and Lex seek refuge in the kitchen.

tigers stalking a reputed hunter. Creating that kind of suspense was a lot of fun; but it was also very difficult to pull off under the circumstances. We had two kids and two raptors, and there was a lot of sneaking around and hiding in the scene." One of the most difficult aspects of the shoot was that a variety of Stan Winston's raptor creations had to be maneuvered within the confines of the set. "Stan and I had to figure out where to hide the raptor operators—it took a lot of people to control two raptors. On the set, it was actually more hilarious than frightening because just under the kids there would be three operators with remote controls, another six operators underneath the camera, twelve operators hiding in the cabinetry. The actors were literally stepping over operators to go through the actions of the scene."

Top left: The kitchen sequence employed a variety of full-size raptors devised by the Stan Winston Studio. *Above:* Operators prepare one of the velociraptors for filming. *Bottom left:* Stalked by a pair of the predatory beasts, Tim hides beneath a kitchen countertop.

Because the choreography of the raptors was of the utmost importance, the kitchen set had actually been designed around the action illustrated in the storyboards and animatics. In reality, a standard-size industrial kitchen would never have accommodated the raptors' maneuvers. "The raptors were eight feet long," noted set designer John Berger. "In a normal-size kitchen, they would have been all the way across the room in only two steps. So, as the design evolved, the kitchen got bigger and bigger. The set also had to be elevated to allow for the raptor puppeteers below." To aid in the design process, Winston had provided the art department with a fifth-scale model of the raptor. "Matching the scale of the raptor model, we built a fifth-scale mockup of the set—which was a very large model for us—to make sure that the raptor would be able to turn all the corners and fit in all the spaces. The model had a clean, white starkness to it, which Steven really liked. He wanted a high-tech look, with some kind of reflective quality to the surfaces."

Panels of brushed aluminum provided a reflective, sterile quality, but also presented a problem when it came time to shoot the sequence. "As the set was being built," said Dean Cundey, "I was in constant consultation with Rick Carter about where the reflective surfaces were going to be and how we could dull them down enough so that they wouldn't be *too* reflective. On the one hand, I welcomed the visual interest they added to the scene. But it was like working in a room of mirrors. We spent a lot of time just trying to hide our lights and camera and operators."

Perhaps no one faced a greater challenge in the sequence than Stan Winston and his team. The action-laden scene would require not only the two fully mechanical, full-size raptor puppets, but also a pair of raptor suits worn by John Rosengrant and Crash McCreery. While the puppets were used primarily for stationary, albeit expressive, beauty shots of the raptors, the suits were put into commission for shots necessitating broad movement and agility. In addition, cable-actuated foot extensions—used in conjunction with a partial suit—would be employed for low-angle walking shots, while raptor leaps would be realized with a variety of positionable stunt puppets.

Coming off their unequivocal success in Hawaii with the sick triceratops, the Stan Winston team had much to live up to when it came time to shoot the raptors in the kitchen. "We went from this wonderful, lovable triceratops that didn't have to do all that much, to the most complicated dinosaur and the most complicated scene in the entire movie for

us to accomplish," Winston observed. "Up to the very last minute we were rehearsing with the raptor team, working out moves based on the animatics that Phil Tippett had shot so that we would be ready when Steven came in with the first unit. And given how complicated these animals were, they worked beautifully. There were little technical problems, but our pit team was so good and so fast that they would be fixed before anybody else realized there was a problem. We were moving like wildfire."

Having successfully finished in the kitchen, the production moved next door to Stage 23 where the interior of the maintenance shed had been constructed. In an attempt to restore the park's power, Ellie goes to the shed where she suffers a nasty encounter with a raptor. Exteriors relating to the sequence had already been filmed in Hawaii. Slated for the sound stage were interior shots of the raptor inside the shed and Ellie's subsequent escape. Like the kitchen set, the maintenance shed interior had been designed with the performance of the raptor a primary consideration. "The set was built over a big pit on the stage so that the raptor could be operated from below," explained John Berger. "Other than that, it was a simple set—basically a maze of concrete floors and concrete walls with pipes coming out of it."

A number of raptor devices were employed for the scene. "We used the insert head for attack shots," Winston revealed, "as well as a full-

Top: Spielberg conceived the kitchen sequence as a terrifying stalk-and-chase scene. The complex actions of the raptors had been prechoreographed in animatics produced by Phil Tippett early in preproduction. *Below:* Lex and Tim hide from the advancing beasts.

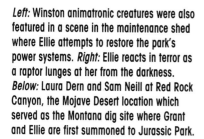

Left: Winston animatronic creatures were also featured in a scene in the maintenance shed where Ellie attempts to restore the park's power systems. *Right:* Ellie reacts in terror as a raptor lunges at her from the darkness. *Below:* Laura Dern and Sam Neill at Red Rock Canyon, the Mojave Desert location which served as the Montana dig site where Grant and Ellie are first summoned to Jurassic Park.

body, locking-joint version that had an articulated head. We also used the walking raptor legs for that sequence, and we were able to get a wonderfully dynamic looking run."

With yet another of the film's most complicated dinosaur sequences in the can, the production moved on to a series of straight live-action scenes at a dig site which both the book and screenplay had set in Montana. Originally, the producers and Spielberg had intended to transport the cast and crew to a Montana location in order to photograph early scenes in which the characters of Grant and Ellie are introduced and the summons from Hammond arrives. On second consideration, however, the filmmakers determined that Red Rock Canyon in the Mojave Desert—just a two-hour drive from Los Angeles—would adequately serve the story. "We discovered that we could save $350,000 by *not* going to Montana," noted Spielberg. "So I decided to compromise, shoot the sequence in Mojave and call it Montana."

"It wasn't as good as Montana would have been," admitted Kathy Kennedy, "but in the scheme of things it worked fine. We brought our consultant on the show, paleontolo-

Clockwise from upper left: Sam Neill, Steven Spielberg and Laura Dern at the Mojave location. / On hand at the site were Don Lessum, founder of The Dinosaur Society and paleontologist Jack Horner. / Grant and Ellie examine the newest find from the paleontological dig.

gist Jack Horner, out to the site to make sure we were setting it up realistically; and he said it looked exactly like the environments he had worked in. So we got his stamp of approval."

By the time the company returned to Universal Studios on Tuesday, September 29, it was already apparent that the production was progressing ahead of its original schedule—an especially remarkable feat considering the creature-intensive nature of the film. Moving forward at breakneck speed, Spielberg clearly was out to prove something. "From the beginning," Spielberg admitted, "I was afraid that a movie like *Jurassic Park* could get away from me. There had been other pictures—

WHY DINO'S BECAME EXTINCT – No. 1

1941, Jaws and *Hook*—where the production simply got away from me and I was dragged behind schedule. I was determined not to let it happen this time. So I walked away from a lot of takes where, on my last picture, I might have stayed for four or five more. And I found that by walking away, I created a discipline—not just for myself, but for the entire crew. The actors knew that we were either going to get it by take five or we weren't going to get it; and everybody rose to the occasion. The actors were as good on their fourth or fifth take as they would have been in a more lax situation at take fifteen; so I wasn't compelled to go any further. That was one of the main reasons we were able to move so fast. Rick Carter kept saying: 'You're too far ahead! I can't keep up with you!' And that was music to my ears."

Although it was Spielberg's determination to finish on time and on budget that drove the production, other factors also contributed to the efficiency of the shoot. Whereas mechanical creatures have been known to bring a production to a painful and screeching halt, Stan Winston's dinosaurs were performing admirably, with little schedule-consuming downtime. Another factor was that Dean Cundey had been constantly on the lookout for ways to shorten setup times between scenes. "My background is in low-budget, nonunion films," Cundey remarked, "where we had twenty-one days to shoot an entire feature. So I developed a working style that enabled me to look at a rehearsal of a scene and come up with a plan that would mean fewer changes and less time between setups. It's a reflex I have developed over the years, and I think it was an aspect of why things went so smoothly."

While beneficial to the production overall, the accelerated pace of the shoot created a pressure-cooker situation for the construction crew. The production schedule was being revised forward almost daily, resulting in ever-tightening construction deadlines. "They drove us absolutely nuts," John Villarino said laughingly. "We like to be so far ahead that we never *see* the production company. But on this show, I think we were actually in some of the shots, standing there finishing up a paint job. Fortunately, this crew worked so well together—production and construction crews—that we were always able to finish on time. It caused some weekends and some nights and some tempers to flare, but the job got done."

The company would spend many of the remaining production days on Stage 27 at Universal. One of two sites where the film's exterior scenes would be staged, the barnlike edifice would be dressed and redressed to represent four distinct areas of Jurassic Park's densely foliaged grounds. The various Stage 27 sets were designed by Marty Kline, with construction supervised by Villarino. Much of the construction effort consisted of dressing the stage with truckloads of real and synthetic vegetation to simulate a dense rain forest. "We brought in real trees," said Villarino, "and also built artificial trees that were sculpted out of foam by Yarik Alfer. We would make a metal or wood cage and then cover it with two-

Exteriors not filmed on location were shot on jungle sets constructed on Hollywood sound stages at Universal Studios and Warner Brothers. To simulate a tropical rain forest on one of the cavernous stages, real vegetation was supplemented with artificial trees made of wood and foam.

One of four jungle settings designed by Marty Kline and constructed on a stage at Universal.

inch-thick foam. We had, at one time, twenty people just painting the trees and tying greens to them—kind of like an assembly line. We used those primarily for the backgrounds. In the foreground we used either real trees, or dead trees with fresh green leaves attached to them."

Among the most compelling—and technically demanding—of the scenes slated to be photographed on Stage 27 was one in which Grant and Tim are literally chased down the length of a giant tree by one of the park tour vehicles. The sequence follows the tyrannosaurus attack on the main road where, deserted by the panic-stricken Donald Gennaro— Hammond's lawyer—Tim and Lex are left alone and injured inside a tour car severely damaged by the enraged animal. In a moment of reprieve granted by the T-rex's pursuit of Malcolm and Gennaro, Grant is able to pull Lex from the car. Before her brother can be retrieved, how- ever, the rex returns to continue its assault on the battered vehicle, ulti- mately pushing it over the edge of a steep road barrier where it makes a precarious landing on a leafy treetop. Grant later climbs the giant tree in order to rescue Tim from the teetering vehicle. When the branches begin to give way under the preponderant weight, Grant and Tim scramble down the tree, the falling car just inches above them throughout their hasty descent.

The scene's exterior setting featured a fifty-foot artificial tree rigged for the car chase by Michael Lantieri, then covered and detailed by the art department and construction crews. Because Spielberg wanted it to appear three times its actual height, the tree was dressed differently on three sides. Positioned at the top of one side, the car would be dropped the available fifty feet, then repositioned at the top of a second, differently dressed side and dropped again. Repeating it once more on the third side, the car would appear to drop a full 150 feet through clever editing.

To devise the complicated rigging for the tree car chase, Lantieri had built the tree first as a fifth-scale model. "I worked with Steven and determined how the car should fall, how it should slip through the branches to create the maximum suspense. The tree had a steel skeleton rigged with joints and hydraulics so that we could control the movement of the branches. Then we skinned it and foamed it and brought in sculptors to make it look like a tree, leaving sockets so that we could plug in real branches and blend them in. For some of the shots that the actors weren't in, we put in real branches and just let this falling, two-thousand-pound car shear them off. Other times we installed hydraulically controlled T-branches that would hold the weight of the car, no matter what happened. We got some really good closeup shots of Sam Neill right under one of those branches as the car slammed into it above his head."

No small amount of faith was required for the actor to participate in the scene. "It was scary," admitted Neill. "To see that car free-falling

A key scene on the jungle set had Grant and Tim scrambling down a tall tree as a falling tour car follows just inches above them. *Far left:* A steel frame with hydraulic branches was devised by Michael Lantieri, then covered with a sculpted tree form and dressed with real and artificial branches. *Left:* Spielberg demonstrates Grant's position at the end of the sequence. *Above:* Grant attempts to rescue Tim who is trapped inside the tour vehicle perched precariously atop the tree.

towards me was really something. But I never felt I was in danger. This was a top crew and I relied on their judgment. If they said the car was going to stop six inches above my head, I was prepared to take their word for it."

Serving double duty, the steel skeleton of the fifty-foot tree was redressed when Stage 27 was reconfigured to represent another area of the park exterior. With the park's security irreparably compromised due to an unscheduled shutdown of the computer system, leaving its prehistoric inhabitants dangerously unsecured, Grant and the children attempt to

Right: The same fifty-foot tree was redressed for a subsequent scene in which Grant, Tim and Lex spend the night in a treetop and awaken to find a gentle brachiosaur grazing on its leaves. *Below:* The three come face to face with the towering sauropod. *Below right:* The full-size head and neck section of the brachiosaur, designed and built by the Stan Winston team.

make their way back to the visitor center on foot. As night falls, they stop to rest, climbing to the top of a tree for safety. In the morning, they are awakened by a gentle brachiosaur grazing at their treetop perch.

Stan Winston Studio had designed and constructed a brachiosaur head and neck for the sequence. "We used a hydraulically operated crane to get the broad movements of her body," said Winston, "with cable and radio controls for the smaller movements of the head—eyes, lids, lips and breathing nostrils. There is interaction between the brachiosaur and the kids. They try to pull a leaf out of her mouth and there is a kind of tug-of-war between them. Then, as she pulls away, you see the full-size animal, which was done as a computer generated element."

Principal photography was nearing its halfway mark by the time the production moved to Stage 28 to film scenes within the Jurassic Park control room, lab and hatchery. Storywise, the rooms were located in the upper level of the visitor center rotunda. Although, in reality, the lower level of the rotunda had been constructed several stages away, set design-er Lauren Cory's concept for the control room reflected the circular motif of that ground floor. "I tried to create a control room that was a combination of masculine, hard lines and the curved lines that had already been established in the building, with everything coming off a radius." For guidance in establishing the high-tech ambience of the room, Cory researched similarly computer-dominated environments at MIT and several theme parks. "Every computer station had to be high-ly personalized, as if some of the top hackers in the world worked there, with all the latest, greatest equipment. The control room also had to have a well-defined, lived-in look because, unlike the rest of the park, these

Computer graphics displays depicting various aspects of the park operation were produced by a team headed by Michael Backes and used on monitors throughout the control room.

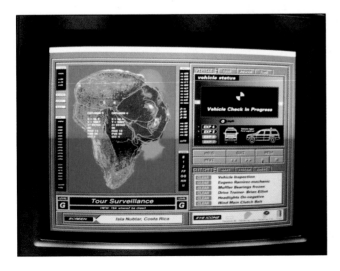

rooms have been up and running for several years." Also influencing the design was the fact that, in the story, the rooms are an integral part of the park tour. "We tried to create the impression that, aside from being functional, these rooms were showpiece sets that were going to be seen by the public. To get that idea across, we combined cold, functional things like acoustical tile with teak beams and stone carvings."

Above: The control room set under construction. Circular viewing ports were incorporated into the set—designed by Lauren Cory—since the control room was conceived to be an integral part of the park tour. *Above right:* John Hammond with game warden Robert Muldoon and control room technician Ray Arnold. *Below right:* From the view deck of the control room, Hammond observes Dennis Nedry, the brilliant but greedy architect of the park's computer systems.

Dominating the control room set was a six-by-eight-foot screen from which control room personnel would monitor the various sectors of the park. Throughout scenes in the control room, this screen would display a variety of graphics depicting, among other things, weather conditions, locations of the animals and breakdowns within the park's security system. For *Jurassic Park,* a dynamic and interactive method was employed to create the graphics, both on the big screen and on the computer monitors at each individual station. A makeshift room was built adjacent to the set, then equipped with a battery of Silicon Graphics and Apple Macintosh computer systems. Stored on computer disks were animations generated over a period of six months by a four-man computer graphics team headed by Michael Backes. Responding to cues received via radio from the set, Backes and his team were able to feed their graphics directly to the appropriate monitors on stage, making it seem as though the actors involved were actually calling up the imagery.

Effectively convincing, the real-time approach to displaying graphics on the on-set computers was made possible by the generous loans of equipment by Silicon Graphics and Apple Computer. "Everything in the set was real," Cory stated. "We couldn't fake any of it, because audiences are so sophisticated now in their knowledge of computers." All told, $875,000 worth of computer hardware loaned by Silicon Graphics, $350,000 worth from Apple and some $500,000 in additional hardware and software went into equipping both the set and off-stage control room.

Adjacent to the control room and laboratory was the hatchery where, early in their tour of Jurassic Park, the visiting scientists witness the emergence of a baby raptor from its egg. Originally, the hatchery sequence was to have featured two of Stan Winston's creations—a hatching triceratops and a somewhat older baby raptor that would playfully crawl up Tim's arm. "The baby triceratops was going to be a simple finger puppet," Winston asserted, "with just its head popping out from the egg. In contrast, the infant raptor crawling up the boy's arm would have been a major effect for us because its whole body would have been seen moving. Eventually, the baby raptor part of the scene was cut, and Steven decided to change the triceratops hatchling to a raptor hatchling."

Still slated as a relatively uncomplicated finger puppet effect, the change from triceratops to raptor was of little concern to Winston—until Spielberg announced his intention to reveal the baby crawling completely outside the eggshell. "We were back to a full dinosaur pup-

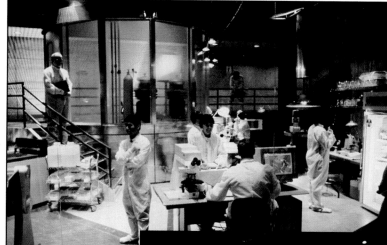

Clockwise from upper left: Nedry steals dinosaur embryos from the embryo storage unit. / The Jurassic Park genetic laboratory. / Featured in the control room was a large viewscreen for park monitoring. / Hammond and the inspection team observe the hatchery activities from a revolving platform. / Muldoon and Arnold monitor the progress of the tour group from the control room.

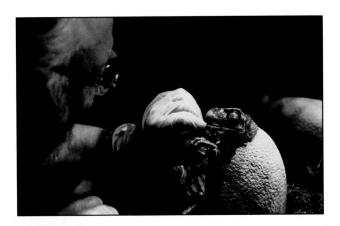

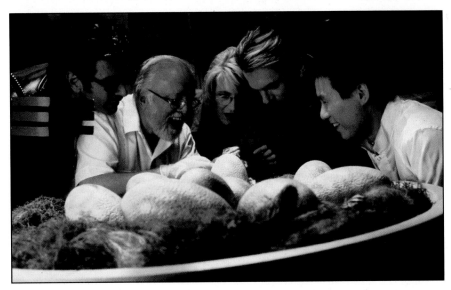

Adjacent to the control room is a hatchery where the scientists observe the birth of a baby velociraptor. *Upper left:* Stan Winston—whose crew constructed the tiny raptor puppet—prepares Sam Neill for the scene. *Above:* The mechanical hatchling was required to punch through a prescored eggshell, then move in newborn-fashion as its full body was revealed. *Left:* Malcolm, Hammond, Ellie, Grant and geneticist Henry Wu witness the emergence of the baby raptor.

pet again," said Winston. "And a little dinosaur puppet was actually harder to do than a big dinosaur puppet, because how do you get all your mechanisms into this tiny thing with spindly arms? Richard Landon volunteered for the job; and although we had originally thought we would have to do it with rod puppeteering and have the rods removed digitally in postproduction, Richard decided to mechanize the thing internally. For the most part, it worked. The tail and head and arms moved, and it had a breathing action. Because of the fineness of the wires Richard had had to use in this tiny thing, its movements were somewhat spastic. But on film it looked very real and totally organic, because that's the way newborns actually move."

It was Tuesday, October 27, when the first unit moved off the Universal lot and onto Warner Brothers' Stage 16 to shoot the tyran-

When the park's security system is deactivated, the freed tyrannosaur attacks the tour vehicles stalled nearby. *Above:* Grant and Lex make their escape, climbing down a steep, vine-covered retaining wall. *Below:* Malcolm, Ellie and Gennaro are searching for Grant, the kids, and the T-rex.

nosaurus rex attack on the stalled tour vehicles carrying the visiting children and luminaries. Seduced by a rival bioengineering firm, and having accepted a great deal of money in exchange for fifteen dinosaur embryos, Dennis Nedry—the brilliant, but nerdish engineer of Jurassic Park's all-encompassing computer control system—executes a total shutdown of the system in order to override security and gain access to the embryo storage vault. With the system down, the automated tour cars stall near the T-rex paddock. More significantly, the shutdown disrupts the flow of high-voltage electricity to the towering fence which serves to contain the fierce animal. Robbed of its electrical punch, the barrier proves ineffectual against the tremendous strength of the T-rex, who tears through the fence and launches an assault on the stranded tour members.

The days on Stage 16 were to be a momentous period in the production schedule for both Stan Winston and Michael Lantieri, and their respective crews. Designed and built by the Winston team and mounted into the set by Lantieri, the full-size, hydraulically actuated tyrannosaur that had been almost two years in the making was finally going to make its debut in front of the cameras.

In part, the significance of that debut lay in the fact that the Winston company had ventured into somewhat unfamiliar territory in realizing the T-rex. Not only was it by far the largest creature the studio had ever produced, it was also the first—by Winston or anyone else—to be mounted on a motion simulator to achieve gross body movements. Furthermore, prior to the *Jurassic Park* project, the Winston team had

The giant predator batters the tour vehicle in which Tim and Lex are trapped. The sequence was photographed on stage at Warner Brothers utilizing Stan Winston's full-size, hydraulic tyrannosaur.

had little experience with the kinds of advanced hydraulics systems necessary to actuate such an enormous creature. Winston's relative inexperience in state-of-the-art hydraulics had, in fact, led him to hire consultant Craig Barr, a veteran of computer-controlled, hydraulically driven amusement park attractions, such as the King Kong ride at Universal Studios in Florida. Barr was to become an invaluable member of the T-rex team.

"Craig's area of expertise was in large-scale hydraulics and their interface with computer systems," Winston explained. "When I first met with him, he basically told me that I was going to need him. And my response was, 'We'll see.' So I hired him on a trial basis, and he soon became an essential part of the project. He had the language to talk to the people at McFadden Systems, who had built our flight simulator, so he was able to help us work out those problems. Craig was also integral in getting us the key people we needed, such as Lloyd Ball who was our hydraulic engineer. Craig turned out to be a real problem solver for us; and as I look back on this job, I know it would not have been nearly the success it was without him."

From the inception of the project, Spielberg had recognized that the T-rex attack had the potential to be the most grueling part of the shoot. Not only would he be dealing with a twenty-foot-tall, thirteen-thousand-pound mechanical creature, the entire sequence was to be played in a drenching rainstorm. Hoping to avoid the static long-shots that characterized previous dinosaur movies, the director burdened

Clockwise: Spielberg shot the attack sequence almost entirely from the confined point-of-view of the children within the car. / Grant uses a flare to divert the animal from Tim and Lex. / Unable to get at the kids inside, the T-rex pushes the disabled vehicle towards a steep drop.

himself even further by determining to present the action primarily from the confined point-of-view of the characters. "We did have shots outside the vehicle to show relative scale between the T-rex and the Explorers," Spielberg said, "but for the most part, the shots are from the inside of the car, looking out. And those are the scariest moments. It is the way *we* would experience the attack if it were really happening. It was more limiting visually to shoot it that way, but I thought it would also be a lot more affecting."

Like the jungle environments at Universal, the Stage 16 set where the T-rex attack would be enacted was designed by Marty Kline to replicate the exteriors shot in Hawaii. "Primarily the set was a large section of road," explained Kline, "with an expanse of the electrical fence on one side, and a rest area and bathroom on the other—and, of course, a lot of jungle in the background. Stage 16 is a huge stage, measuring approximately 135 by 240 feet. In fact, I think we had more room on that stage than we'd had on location."

It was the massive size of Stage 16—one of the biggest sound stages Hollywood had to offer—that had prompted the move from Universal to Warner Brothers. In addition, the structure was particularly well suited to the action of the T-rex attack sequence because it was a tank stage—a stage with flooring built over a six-foot-deep concrete pit. "We took out a portion of that floor to create an edge for shots of the tour vehicle rolling over the cliff during the attack," Kline explained. "Another area of flooring was removed to create a mud pit. The car was placed in the pit, on inner tubes, so that we could create the impression of the vehicle being pressed into the mud by the weight of the dinosaur."

Most importantly, the concrete pit afforded a solid mounting place for the T-rex simulator platform. Working closely with Stan Winston, Joss Geiduschek of Michael Lantieri's special effects group had designed a tower that could be mounted beneath the stage floor to provide support for the motion simulator rig. "We had to come up with a way to support the weight and all the g-forces that would be generated when it was moving," Lantieri said. "One of the things Steven had

Left: Winston and his crew built various versions of the T-rex, including separate walking legs coupled with a closeup head and neck assembly. *Right:* Grant and Lex sit motionless in order to avoid detection by the advancing carnivore.

emphasized was that he wanted the T-rex to move *fast*—and that meant that a tremendous amount of force was going to be generated. If we had just put the motion simulator on the stage floor, it would have torn that floor up the first time it was activated. So we designed an air-bearing system that went underneath the simulator to spread that weight around structurally. Our tower was drilled into bedrock, seven feet below the stage, with concrete piles surrounding it, and the T-rex rig was bolted to that."

The tower structure was also instrumental in moving the T-rex rig from one position on the stage to another—a difficult, several-hour job that, fortunately, was necessitated only four times during the course of production. "We'd had meetings for months, just to figure out how many shots we could get in one position so we wouldn't be moving this thing over and over again. To reposition her on the stage, we had to loosen the bolts in our tower and basically glide the T-rex along the floor on air bearings, which took a tremendous amount of pressure and air volume to accomplish."

Despite the complexity of its mounting and mechanical systems, the tyrannosaur performed superbly—although not precisely in the manner anticipated. During preproduction, the Stan Winston Studio had expended a great deal of time and effort in developing a computerized waldo system that would enable the T-rex team to record prechoreographed movements—movements that could then be repeated precisely for numerous takes with a simple pressing of a button. In the

The Winston team also devised a computerized waldo system that enabled the T-rex operators to preprogram moves so they could be easily repeated on demand.

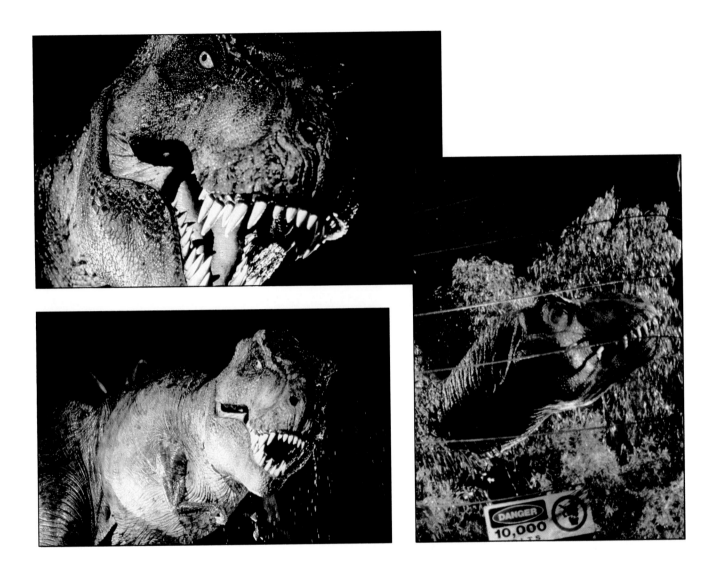

The animatronic T-rex in action on the set.

on-the-fly atmosphere of the movie set, however, Winston and his crew discovered that it was more expedient, and even more dynamic, to puppeteer the creature manually for each take. "There was an advantage in the spontaneity of the moment," Winston commented. "Sometimes there would be mistakes that actually made the performance of the T-rex look more real. We still used the programming capability in situations where the animal had to hit a mark exactly. But when the T-rex had to *act*, we did it on the spot—and it was wonderful. Steven would say, 'Get yourself a cup of tea' and the T-rex would go get a cup of tea. It roared and hit cars and slammed into things and acted its ass off."

Although not used as extensively as planned, the waldo system was invaluable in executing a scene in which Malcolm is pushed through a restroom wall on the nose of the tyrannosaur. Full-body views of the T-rex's advance on the mathematician as he runs toward the shelter were to be computer generated, while Winston's mechanical insert head was employed for the shot of Malcolm crashing through the wall astride the animal's face. To avoid human error in the potentially dangerous stunt, the creature's programmable capability was utilized. "The T-rex had to hit its mark exactly," said Winston. "We started by rehearsing its move from point A to point B, and we logged that move in. Then we worked with the stuntman, who was harnessed to a flying rig, to determine exactly what his position should be. When it came time to do the shot, we just pushed a button and the T-rex executed her move precisely, crashing through the breakaway wall of the restroom set with the stuntman on her nose. It was a perfect example of where the recordability of the animal was a necessity."

While the restroom wall crash was deemed too dangerous to be performed by Jeff Goldblum, the T-rex attack sequence did afford the actor his best opportunity to get up-close and personal with one of the mechanical dinosaurs. "It was a pleasure and a privilege to work with the dinosaurs," Goldblum asserted. "I *loved* dinosaurs when I was a kid. I remember having a book about a kid who found an egg in his backyard that turned out to be a baby triceratops. And I was always astounded by the dinosaur bone collection I passed on my way to art class at the Carnegie Museum every Saturday. So, for me, it was thrilling to see these dinosaurs come to life."

In a drenching rainstorm, Malcolm confronts the T-rex on the main road.

Left: Creature creator Stan Winston with his tyrannosaur. *Below:* The animatronic beast was carefully maintained on the set and its paint job touched up as required. *Bottom:* A major challenge faced by the T-rex team was the incessant rain which soaked into the creature's foam latex skin, necessitating frequent towel-dryings between takes.

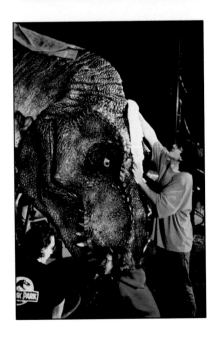

In the end, the most problematic element of the T-rex shoot did not stem directly from the rig's complex electronics or high-tech hydraulic systems. Rather, it was the constant downpour of water that wreaked havoc for the dinosaur team. Because of the rain machines which were operating almost continuously on the set, and the ultra-absorbent properties of foam rubber, the T-rex retained tremendous amounts of water in the course of a single shooting day. Not only was the water damaging to the foam rubber skin, the resulting additional weight—which was considerable—disrupted the creature's finely tuned and balanced mechanisms.

Winston had foreseen the problems water could create for his animatronic creation. "We had *planned* for the water, because we knew from the script that this scene took place in a rainstorm. We had attacked the problem early on, coming up with new and better ways to waterproof foam rubber. But we found that, no matter how much we waterproofed it, water always found a way in. So we had decided more than a year before photography started that we would go out of our way on the set to make sure that it rained in front of the creature, or in back of the creature, but never right *on* the creature. Needless to say, once we got to shooting it, that concept faded away and we ended up drenching this thing, which created enormous complications. We had to run in after every shot and dry it down. Eventually, the skins would soak up the water

Above: Winston art department supervisor John Rosengrant airbrushes the inside of the T-rex mouth. *Below:* Game warden Robert Muldoon stalks a raptor which has escaped its pen.

anyway; so we had teams come in at the end of the day after shooting and stay all night just to dry this thing out with big dryers. Also, certain components in the motion base shorted out and got waterlogged. We were in a constant state of repair and upkeep. It was hellacious for us, but the T-rex looked great on film—and that's really all that mattered."

The near-continuous downpour was an annoyance for the human participants in the shoot, as well. "It made it harder to work," Dean Cundey recalled, "because our equipment was always wet and we were traipsing in mud, even after they had turned the rain off. But the advantage, from a cinematography standpoint, was that it was a nice visual device. As we would roll the camera on any particular shot, it was interesting to see how the rain kept the frame alive. Once the rain was off, it would suddenly go dead and we would see where the trees ended and the phony night sky began. So it definitely added a dramatic element, even though it was bothersome."

Due in no small part to the reliability of the animatronic T-rex, Spielberg managed to emerge from the attack sequence another four days ahead of schedule. "I think we all shared the motivation to be out of the wet weather," Spielberg observed. "It was very uncomfortable for the actors and crew—even with the wet weather gear, we were all bone-soaked by the end of the day. So all of us pulled to get out of there early. But I didn't have to compromise the sequence at all. In fact, I actually added shots that hadn't been in the storyboards or the animatics."

After the arduous T-rex shoot, three dinosaur sequences remained to be shot back at Universal. Still to be filmed was the scene in which Robert Muldoon, Jurassic Park's game warden, engages a raptor in a contest of hunting prowess—and loses. Also scheduled was the scene in which Dennis Nedry meets his death in an encounter with a dilophosaur. Finally, there was the climactic stalk-and-chase sequence in the visitor center featuring a pair of raptors and a return engagement by the tyrannosaurus rex.

Muldoon's death was staged in

the again-revamped jungle set on Stage 27. As scripted, the veteran hunter stalks a raptor through the jungle and, smelling victory, carefully lines the animal up in his gun sight. Just as he is about to pull the trigger, however, he hears a movement behind him and turns to see a second raptor, poised and ready to attack. Granted only a split second in which to comprehend the one-upsmanship realized by the intelligent beasts, Muldoon is killed.

The scene required Stan Winston team member John Rosengrant to perform inside the raptor suit, and also featured the counterweighted insert head operated by Craig Caton. "There is a shot over Muldoon's shoulder as he is sighting up the raptor," said Caton, "and that was John in the suit. Then the camera dollies past Muldoon and rack-focuses into some bushes, right behind his shoulder. That's where you see the second raptor. I was standing there strapped into the raptor insert head, and the crew had dressed jungle all around me so I wouldn't be seen. They threw camouflage netting over my head and put vegetation all around me. I was operating the raptor with one hand, and holding a little two-inch monitor in my other hand so that I could watch what I was doing in the scene."

Nedry's deadly encounter with the venom-spitting dilophosaur also employed Winston's mechanical creations. On his way to meet a boat at the island harbor, Nedry runs his jeep off the road and into a muddy embankment. Hopelessly stuck, he is attempting to winch the vehicle out of the mud when a small, deceptively benign-looking dinosaur approaches. More irritated than alarmed, Nedry tries to shoo the animal away as it nears him. Finally within range, the spitter flares her cowl and expectorates venom into the man's eyes. Blinded, Nedry stumbles to his vehicle, slamming the door against further attack—or so he thinks. Within moments, the distinctive hoot of the spitter is heard inside the car, and with her cowl vibrating angrily, the animal attacks.

For the scene, Winston's team had created a full-body dilophosaur puppet, with interchangeable heads to accommodate specific actions and the various configurations of the animal's cowl. Hopping insert legs were also constructed for the spitter's initial approach. "The first image you see in the sequence," noted Winston, "is the creature hopping by with Nedry in the background. Those insert legs worked beautifully, but we never got a good walk out of the full-body puppet—so you never see the full animal actually walking up to Nedry. But that was one of those mistakes that ended up working to the film's advantage; because as it is

Velociraptor suits worn by performers, full-size actuated puppets, positionable stunt puppets and a counterweighted raptor head and neck rig were all employed to realize the game warden's death scene.

now, the animal is just suddenly there. Every time you see her, she is closer; but you never see how she got there. It's a now-you-see-her, now-you-don't situation, which worked beautifully for the scene."

The last major sequence to be filmed was the grand finale in the visitor center rotunda. Constructed on Universal's Stage 12, the rotunda consisted of a main entrance hall where two life-size dinosaur skeletons were posed in mock battle, a large circular staircase, and a dining area adorned with a painted mural depicting life in the Jurassic era. One of the key sets in the show, the visitor center had been designed as a model

Clockwise: A dilophosaur puppet built by the Winston team. / Attempting to smuggle his stolen dinosaur embryos off the island, Dennis Nedry encounters the seemingly harmless, yet lethal creature. / The puppeteering crew prepares to shoot a scene with the dilophosaur puppet. / One full-body dilophosaur was built and used with three separate, interchangeable heads.

of classic simplicity. "We liked the idea of a rotunda," said Rick Carter, "a simple space that was something like a museum. The visitor center is basically a jumping-off place for the tour, so what had to be conveyed there was a sense of what we have learned about dinosaurs up to this point in time. That's why we decided to put the skeletal structures of the T-rex and the alamosaurus in the center. Other than the mural in the dining room—which was painted by Doug Henderson, a renowned dinosaur illustrator—we didn't decorate the set with too much dinosaur imagery. We didn't want to take away from the real dinosaurs the audience would be seeing later."

Set designer Paul Sonski was charged with developing the interior. "The visitor center was a kind of monument to dinosaurs," said Sonski, "so it had an entrance that was reminiscent of a temple. Its main function was to emphasize the dinosaurs. To support that idea, we included bone forms in the structure of the stairway and fossils in the decoration of the columns."

Although impressive, the rotunda was one of the most difficult sets in which to film, largely due to its circular design. "It had to be shot with very wide lenses," observed Dean Cundey, "because it would have been a shame not to show off such a large, creatively designed set. But in photographing it that way, we were also opening ourselves up to showing all the flaws in it—the fact that it was built on stage, with no real sky or scenery outside. Placing the lights was also a painstaking process. Where can you hide lights when you are doing a 180-degree dolly move that

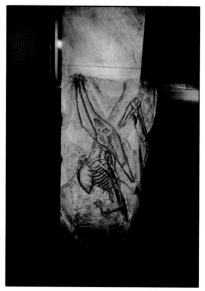

Clockwise from upper left: The visitor center rotunda under construction at Universal. / Steven Spielberg and Sam Neill confer on the completed set. / The rotunda would serve as the setting for a climactic battle between the T-rex and a pair of raptors. Because the animals would be computer generated images composited into the scene, story poles were used to stand in for the creatures when background footage was shot. / Foam sculpted column for rotunda of visitor center.

shows the entire set all in one shot? One of the reasons I had worked so closely with Rick Carter ahead of time was so that we could look for those kinds of problems and make sure there was a way to solve them."

With Muldoon and Nedry both dead, and Hammond and the injured Malcolm safely ensconced inside a bunker, Ellie, Grant and the children seek refuge in the control room, determined to bring the park back on-line and thus reactivate the phone system so that they can call for help. They succeed, but their joy in the knowledge that help is on its way is deflated when a raptor leaps through a control room window. A

Left: Grant, Ellie and the children end up atop the skeletal display in the rotunda after being chased through the control room and visitor center by raptors. *Center:* The visitor center dining room featured a large mural depicting life in the Jurassic era. *Below:* Standing skeletal replicas of a tyrannosaur and alamosaur were custom-made for the production and rigged to collapse segmentally on cue.

Laura Dern clings to one of the dinosaur skeletons during the rotunda shoot.

variety of Winston's raptor creations were employed for the ensuing chase through the building air duct system which ends with the characters atop the giant dinosaur skeletons in the visitor center lobby.

The chase sequence was one of the most physical for the actors. "I had to jump onto the skeleton in the rotunda," Laura Dern recalled. "Then the raptor jumped onto it, breaking it in half. So I was hanging from the tail of it, upside down. At one point during all of this, I turned to Steven and said, 'And I wanted to be an actress. . .' I mean, I was hanging from a dinosaur bone! It was a really different experience, and a lot of fun."

As originally scripted, the onslaught was to end with Grant, at the controls of a big platform crane, maneuvering the raptor into the jaws of the skeletal T-rex where it would be crushed to death. Principal photography was well underway when Spielberg revised the ending so that the raptor would become the prey of the living T-rex instead. "When I saw how wonderful and commanding the T-rex was," Spielberg commented, "I began to feel that the audience would be disappointed if she didn't make a return visit. Also, it seemed fitting to me, since this movie is really about nature succeeding and man failing, that it is the T-rex that saves the day."

The revised ending was also prompted, in part, by the success ILM was enjoying in creating their computer generated tyrannosaur. Mounting the massive, real-time T-rex on the rotunda set would not have been a viable option. "Stan's T-rex, with the simulator and everything, weighed several thousand pounds," Kathy Kennedy observed. "So it was not something that we could easily move around. Also, the visitor center set had not been built to accommodate the T-rex. So all of the T-rex shots at the end *had* to be CG. It was kind of a scary, seat-of-the-pants decision, but we had about a month to prepare for it."

Spielberg, not surprisingly, had trepidations about turning over so much of the climax of his film to computer animation that would not be completed until well into postproduction. "I didn't know if it would work, but ILM displayed confidence that they could do it. All I had to go on was their word—but I had relied very heavily on ILM's word throughout the entire production."

Above: A raptor bursts through a ceiling grate into the visitor center air duct system where Grant and Ellie have taken refuge with Tim and Lex. *Left:* Spielberg lines up a shot on one of the velociraptors.

You ain't nothin' but a sauropod.

ELVISAURUS

The new approach toward the end sequence meant that more raptor shots would have to be achieved with computer graphics as well, due to the raptor's direct interaction with the T-rex. Considerably more expensive than utilizing the animatronic puppets, the additional CG shots were feasible from a budgetary standpoint because of the savings generated by Spielberg's early completion of principal photography. "Steven chose to put that savings into more computer graphics," Gerald Molen commented. "The CG work ILM was doing was phenomenal. Even if he had not been ahead of schedule, he still would have made the decision to do the new ending with CG, because it was going to make the picture that much better. But since he *was* so far ahead, he was in a wonderful position to say, 'This is what I'm going to do.' "

Principal photography wrapped on Monday, November 30, 1992—one day after the Thanksgiving break and an astonishing twelve days ahead of schedule. Through unrelenting determination, Spielberg had more than achieved his goal to retain tight control of the production. It was a stellar accomplishment. "I probably drove everyone to the brink of insanity in order to complete this movie on budget and on schedule," Spielberg admitted. "Ending *ahead* of schedule was a bonus. Part of it was my determination, but I have to give credit where credit is due. If Stan Winston's dinosaurs hadn't worked, we'd still be shooting. If Michael Lantieri's physical effects had not functioned, we'd still be shooting. If Dean Cundey had not accomplished more than fifteen camera setups per day, we'd still be shooting. So there were a lot of contributing factors.

"The last time I worked this fast was on *Raiders of the Lost Ark,* which I brought in fourteen days ahead of schedule. But we actually achieved something more with *Jurassic Park*; because on this movie we had scheduled thirty-five second unit days, and I incorporated all but two of those days into the first unit schedule. I got very jealous of the second unit's work and I thought: 'Well, we're here—why throw it to them? Let's get these four shots now, rather than having second unit come in next week and relight the same thing.' So not only did we come in twelve days ahead of schedule on the first unit, we sort of scarfed up the second unit as well. And I'm really proud of that."

Coming in so far ahead of schedule, *and* on budget, was a producer's dream come true. "It's a rare thing to happen in this business," affirmed Molen, "so it was very gratifying. And it can be accounted for by the fact that we were so well prepared to begin with. Then, during production, we had a very creative producer in Kathy Kennedy who was able to work side by side with Steven and help him to keep things moving. Most of all, we had a director whose heart and soul was in this project. All of that made for a winning formula."

Perhaps no one involved in the *Jurassic Park* project was in a better position to appreciate Spielberg's accomplishment than fellow director Richard Attenborough. "Steven should be *barred* from the Director's Guild," Attenborough said laughingly. "He is a menace, an absolute menace! Now the rest of us are really going to have to pull our socks up, aren't we?"

With the wrapping of production, Stan Winston Studio had come to the completion of an assignment they had started nearly three years earlier. Like Spielberg, Winston came out of the *Jurassic Park* experience with a justifiable sense of pride. "This movie was the first time I could sit back and watch the dailies and think to myself, 'God, we did a fabulous job.' Not everything worked perfectly, and not every single shot Steven conceived of were we able to do. But it was still an amazing feat. People are going to see this movie and be entertained by these dinosaurs, which is what the movie is all about. This movie *is* Jurassic Park, as Hammond envisioned it. The dinosaurs are there, they are real, and people are going to leave the theater almost believing that dinosaurs are living amongst us—and that somehow Steven Spielberg found them and shot a movie around them."

Michael Lantieri and his crew had also come to the end of a long and arduous road. "This movie was harder than any other two put together. It was just overwhelmingly difficult. But the results on the screen were well worth it. Steven has such a great eye, he takes whatever you give him and makes it look great. I think the big question in all of our minds now is—where do we go from here? After doing something this big, what's left?"

Others were pondering the same question. Although an enormous amount of work remained to be done in postproduction, the completion of production signaled the end of *Jurassic Park* for Rick Carter, Dean Cundey, the cast and virtually every member of the film crew. To a man—and woman—the experience had been a rewarding one characterized by camaraderie and the sense of a job well done. "I couldn't have been more delighted with the people I was working with," Sam Neill

Universal heralded Steven Spielberg's completion of principal photography well ahead of schedule by placing full-page ads in the motion picture trade papers.

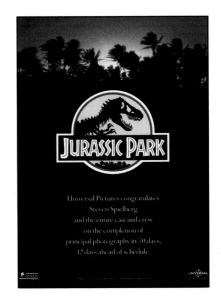

The cast and crew of *Jurassic Park* on the T-rex set at Warner Brothers.

commented. "We got along well; and even though it was a long shoot, it seemed too short by the end. It was one of those good life experiences."

Jurassic Park had been a significant experience for Richard Attenborough, as well. Not only had it ended an informal retirement from acting—at least temporarily—the film had been the long-awaited opportunity to work with a director whose work he held in the highest regard. "Frankly, the year my film, *Gandhi,* was up against Steven's *E.T.,* I was certain that not only would *E.T.* win, but that it *should* win. It was inventive, powerful, wonderful. I make more mundane movies. There are stories that interest me, and I use cinema to tell them. But Steven makes movies because they are movies—and does so magically. When the history of cinema is written over these decades, Steven Spielberg will be heralded as an innovative, exciting, blistering talent."

That blistering talent was already looking ahead to his next project— *Schindler's List,* the true account of a man who saved over one thousand Jews from Hitler's final solution. With *Schindler* scheduled to begin filming in Europe just weeks after the end of *Jurassic Park*'s production schedule, Spielberg would leave the day-to-day responsibilities of *Jurassic's* postproduction in the able hands of Kathleen Kennedy, keeping tabs on the effort by phone and returning from Europe in time for preview screenings and a final polish of the film.

Still to be accomplished in postproduction were Michael Kahn's edit—an ongoing process Kahn and Spielberg had initiated during principal photography—and John Williams's scoring of the completed movie. At Skywalker Ranch in northern California, Gary Rydstrom and Richard Hymns would supervise the creation of sound effects, while the final sound mix would be overseen by Spielberg's longtime friend and associate, George Lucas.

One more thing remained. Stan Winston Studio had inhabited Jurassic Park with living, breathing dinosaurs: raptors that were swift and terrible; a triceratops that was sweetly affecting; a venom-spitting dilophosaur; a terrifyingly real tyrannosaurus rex. But amongst the dynamic scenes featuring this array of prehistoric wildlife were moments that were strangely barren. Characters marveled at the sight of a grazing brachiosaur in the distance—but, as yet, no brachiosaur appeared in the scene. A gallimimus herd was spotted galloping across a tropical plain—but, as yet, the scene revealed nothing but an empty Hawaiian landscape. Grant, Ellie and the children stared in fearful amazement as the T-rex entered the rotunda to feast upon a snarling raptor—but, as yet, the climactic encounter could only be imagined.

At Industrial Light and Magic, Dennis Muren, Phil Tippett and a top-notch team of computer animators stood ready, after months of preparation, to apply the final stroke of genius that would fully realize John Hammond's dream of Jurassic Park.

PART THREE

POST-
PRODUCTION

Officially, postproduction on *Jurassic Park* began in December 1992 and extended until the film's June 11 release date. However, the period was not so much a distinct phase as it was a culmination of an ongoing process. Many of the postproduction tasks had been in the works throughout production and even preproduction: Industrial Light and Magic, working in cooperation with dinosaur supervisor Phil Tippett, had initiated development of their computer generated dinosaurs nearly two years before postproduction commenced; likewise, the sound editors at Skywalker Sound had been engaged in the collection and recording of various sound effects from the time they had first landed the *Jurassic* assignment a year earlier; and, although the editing of the film was technically slated as a postproduction endeavor, editor

This page: Paleontologist Mike Greenwald, Herpetologist Jacques Gauthier, *Jurassic Park* dinosaur supervisor Phil Tippett and paleontologist Rob Long meet to discuss dinosaur behavior and movement.

Michael Kahn had labored throughout principal photography in order to deliver a rough cut within days after the shoot had wrapped.

Because Spielberg was about to begin shooting *Schindler's List* in Europe, it was important to expedite the editing of *Jurassic Park*—a task that was facilitated by the well-prepared nature of the shoot, as well as the editor's longstanding association with its director. Having served as editor on all but one of Steven Spielberg's films since *Close Encounters of the Third Kind*, Kahn was well acquainted with the director's editorial style. "One of the great things about working on a Spielberg movie is that Steven shoots a lot of coverage," Kahn noted. "He shoots enough pieces so that he will have options when he gets into the editing room. He also has a great editing sense in that he doesn't fall in love with every piece of film. If something works, fine; but if it doesn't, it's out. Generally, Steven and I are on the same wavelength in those decisions. After being together for so long, we don't have to talk a lot in the editing room. I understand what he wants."

The editing process had begun during production with Spielberg and Kahn meeting several times a week—most often in the evenings after the day's shooting had ended. "We put the dailies in continuity form, then ran them and made notes about the takes Steven wanted to use. Usually, after he was through shooting a scene, I would put it together right away so that he could make a decision as to whether or not he needed to pick up additional shots. He would determine if the performances and the structure of the scenes were working. Those basic decisions were made very early—which takes to use, how to pace the scene, the rhythm of the scene, what slant we wanted to put on things. It was a very exciting time in the process because both of us couldn't *wait* to see how a scene was going to come together." Subsequent refinements were made once the individual scenes were roughed out. "We would run the film reel by reel and decide what trims we wanted to make and how the show should be paced. It all went very quickly. Some directors want to play with a movie forever, but Steven doesn't dillydally—he gets right in there, and he knows when it is right."

Individual sequences were then strung together to create a coherent whole. "From there it was a matter of building in the transitions from scene to scene. We also had to determine the movie's running time. We weren't concerned with getting it down to under two hours, or any other arbitrary time limit. We were just looking for how it played—if it played best at two hours, it would be two hours; if it played best at two hours and ten minutes, then we would shoot for that. There really wasn't too much trimming to be done, because even in rough cut form there was very little fat in the show."

Absent only the computer graphics elements that would continue to be added until just days before the film's release, a more or less finalized version of *Jurassic Park* was delivered to the sound editors at Skywalker Ranch for sound mixing in early January. By the middle of February, Michael Kahn was in Poland, already turning his attention to Spielberg's new project. As he had on previous outings, Kahn found the collaboration with Spielberg on *Jurassic Park* to be a rewarding one. "Steven and I are a good team and we have fun together. We both enjoy the editing process. I like to think that *Jurassic Park* is going to be a tremendous hit, and that is a good feeling, of course. But the joy is in the process, whether or not the film is a success. You can never tell, going in, if a movie is going to be a hit or not—so you'd better have a good time doing it. And if people like it, that's even better."

Unlike Michael Kahn, who had essentially closed the book on his *Jurassic Park* involvement, Industrial Light and Magic and the Phil Tippett Studio were just hitting their strides by the time post-production started. The task of creating computer generated dinosaurs, never before attempted, had demanded an exhaustive gearing-up process—

Above: Randy Dutra animates a raptor puppet for the kitchen sequence during the animatic phase of production. *Left:* Editor Michael Kahn (far right), longtime Spielberg collaborator, edited *Jurassic Park* with (from left) Patrick Crane, Assistant Editor, Alan Cody, Assistant Editor, and Michael Fallavollita, Apprentice Editor.

Visual effects supervisor Dennis Muren, effects co-supervisor Mark Dippe, animators Steve Williams and Eric Armstrong review CG animation of the T-rex.

traditional stop-motion animators had had to get up to speed in the unfamiliar arena of digital technology; computer animators, accustomed to sitting at keyboards, had been required to sharpen their animation skills through mime training; new hardware to interface the two separate disciplines had had to be developed and built; existing output systems had had to be maximized to improve their efficiency; standard software packages had been upgraded, and entirely new software capabilities had been explored. "At the time *Jurassic Park* came along," noted computer graphics animator Steve Williams, "creating computer generated creatures that had been dead for 150 million years wasn't so much a question of *capability* as it was a matter of sweat. It just took an enormous amount of work."

Such an all-out effort had been necessitated by the expanded role of computer animation in the film since the early development phase when Spielberg and company had first been bowled over by ILM's CG test of a tyrannosaurus rex. At the inception of the project, the director had not even contemplated computer animation as a viable option for creating *Jurassic Park*'s dinosaurs. "I hadn't been very aware of the technology until *Terminator 2* came out," Spielberg admitted. "I was so impressed with the work ILM had done on that film, I thought it was possible that *someday* they might be able to create three-dimensional, live-action characters through computer graphics. But I didn't think it would happen this soon."

Nor did ILM. Even after their participation in the project had been solicited, principals at ILM and Amblin assumed that the CG involvement would be limited to shots of the gallimimus herd—a sequence particularly well suited to computer animation—and a handful of digital rod removals from shots featuring Stan Winston's cable-operated puppets. But with advancements in digital technology—advancements first hinted at by the stunning T-rex tests—the computer graphics assignment had grown to a substantial fifty-two shots. These shots included full-body medium and close shots of the tyrannosaur in the main road attack sequence, shots of the brachiosaur, both in the initial tour sequence and in a later scene in which the computer generated animal would be intercut with footage of Winston's full-size animatronic head, and a variety of raptor shots interspersed throughout the film. Most significantly, the entire end sequence, featuring a major battle between the T-rex and a pair of raptors, was to be created solely through full-motion dinosaur computer generated imagery.

In scope, complexity and subject matter, it was a task of daunting proportions, far more challenging than the computer graphics effects in *Terminator 2* that had so impressed Spielberg—and the entire filmmaking community. The then state-of-the-art digital technology that had produced *T2*'s liquid metal T-1000 had involved building and animating a wire-frame computer model of the character, utilizing data obtained through laser scanning of actor Robert Patrick. Texture map-

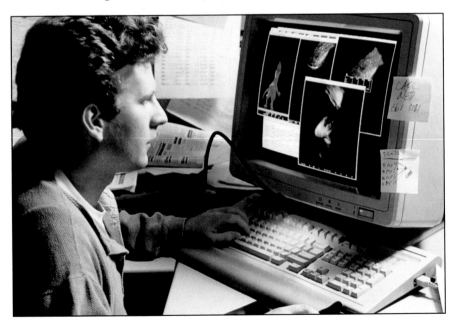

ILM CG supervisor Alex Seiden works on texture details for the computer generated raptor in the kitchen sequence.

ping, a technique to apply specific characteristics onto the wire-frame model, was then employed to create a metallic surface. While the results were dazzling—marking a major advancement in digital effects—the computer generated T-1000 represented only the first baby steps in creating organic, living creatures through computer animation. *Jurassic Park* would require an all-out run.

Of primary concern was producing a photorealistic appearance for the dinosaurs. Whereas the T-1000 had featured only a basic metallic sheen, the dinosaurs in *Jurassic Park* would require all the myriad physical details present in nature in order to read as "real" on the screen. "The T-1000 worked very well," noted assistant visual effects co-supervisor Mark Dippe, "but it wasn't a fleshy creature. It was a metallic thing, so there weren't issues such as: 'Is the metal breathing? When he walks, do his thigh muscles vibrate a little bit?' For *Jurassic Park*, we had to create the appearance of living, breathing dinosaur skin. We came up with texture maps for all the surface detail—the reptilian bumps, the sheen, water lines, dirt, little shiny spots from where they rub on trees, wet eyes, yellow teeth. We were dealing with a level of realism that was way beyond anything we had ever done before." That realism was particularly crucial since Spielberg intended to feature extended, lingering shots of the CG dinosaurs. "There were shots where the camera was on these creatures for twenty seconds at a time—which was very bold of Steven, but that's a

ILM CG animator Steve Price at work.

long time to make any kind of effect hold up."

In addition to the variety of texture maps that would simulate the appearance of skin, the illusion of a supporting understructure of bone and musculature also had to be created in the CG models. Toward that end, software programs such as Sock—originally implemented for *T2*—and Enveloping were developed. Sock was a program that joined the individual network of points—called a patch-mesh—which made up each major anatomical segment of the dinosaur computer model. "We could take all the separate patch-meshes for the various parts of the body—the foot, shin, thigh, hip, belly—animate them, and then run Sock to connect them together into one smooth, continuous body."

While Sock was a means to join individual patch-meshes, Enveloping enabled the computer animators to move points in the *interior* of the patch-mesh to simulate the bulging and compressing of muscles. "Once we got that technique working," said Dippe, "we had control of the entire skin. So as the animal was running, we would see the muscles bulging, we could create breathing effects and we could achieve really smooth transitions as each part of the body twisted or turned."

Among the other advances implemented for *Jurassic Park* was a new animation program offered by SoftImage, a maker of computer software. The new software proved to be a vast improvement on the standard hierarchical animation programs previously employed. "SoftImage

CG animator Geoff Campbell observes as Jeanie Cunningham composites a raptor rotunda shot and Tien Trwong completes a T-rex main road composite.

Top Left: A T-rex armature employed in Tippett's animatics, which were rough versions of key action scenes, choreographed and then shot in video.

DIDs—dinosaur input devices—were devised to provide the stop motion animators at the Tippett Studio a means to more easily interface with the computer generated dinosaur models. *Below left:* Stuart Ziff wires encoders for one of the DID puppets. *Below right:* System designers Craig Hayes and Bart Trickel with the T-rex DID.

allowed us to create dinosaur motion in a more natural way," explained Dippe. "In hierarchical computer animation, we would build a human body, for example, rooting the body at the hips and then attaching the chest, shoulders, head and neck in order. So if we rotated the hips, everything above the hips would rotate as well. But what if we wanted this body to walk like John Wayne, with the hips rotating and the head staying straight ahead? Then we would have to go in and rotate the head back by hand. Hierarchical animation is a pain because it requires constant adjusting. SoftImage allowed us to treat the model more physically—we could make a move and the animation program would automatically adjust all the other angles. We still had to go in and make minor adjustments by hand, but it was light years ahead of the old method."

In addition to the development of software, the project required new hardware—most significantly, the DID, a dinosaur input device designed in a cooperative effort between Phil Tippett and ILM. The DID consisted of an armature equipped with encoders at individual pivot points that enabled movements to be recorded and translated into a wire-frame figure on a computer monitor. Primarily, the DID had been devised to provide Tippett and his team of stop-motion animators a familiar, hands-on means of manipulating computer models. "The DID was a really good merging of two technologies—stop-motion and computer animation," commented visual effects supervisor Dennis Muren.

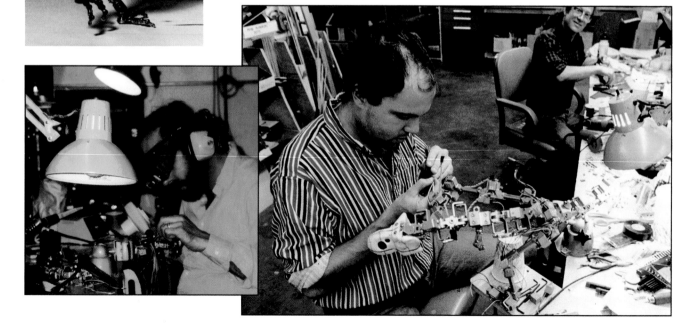

The DID animation team: Phil Tippett, Jules Tippett, Tom St. Amand, Stuart Ziff, Craig Hayes, Bart Trickel, Randy Dutra and Adam Valdez.

"Phil and I had actually discussed building something like this three or four years ago—a device that was built from the stop-motion point of view—because computers are still so hard to use. So instead of forcing stop-motion animators to learn computers, we came up with this hybrid device which was something they could grab and move. Phil's team built the hardware part of it and then we came up with the software. That was a very big deal, just figuring out how we could get all of the data from this moving shape into a usable format that could be viewed on the screen and then rendered."

Initially, Tippett's DID animation team and the ILM computer animators worked side by side. However, as the project grew in complexity, the CG sequences were divided between the two teams with ILM doing two thirds of the shots and Tippett one third. ILM's shots included the gallimimus stampede requiring over 120 dinosaur elements. "It became clumsy to mix the two approaches within one sequence," said Muren. "It made a lot more sense to split it. ILM wound up doing the end sequence in the rotunda, as well as the tour sequence with the brachiosaur, the T-rex chasing the jeep, and the galli stampede. Phil's team concentrated on the main road attack and the raptors in the kitchen."

The first computer generated dinosaur featured in the film is the brachiosaur spotted by the group of scientists early in their tour of the park. Background plates for the scene had been shot by an ILM film crew in Hawaii. "There was a lot of pressure on the set in Hawaii," recalled Muren. "We lost the sun a few times; so we were in a rush to get everything done, which meant we kind of made things up as we went along. I've worked with Steven enough to know that it isn't really a good idea to plan things too much, because he gets a lot of his ideas right on the set. For example, one of the neatest shots in that tour scene was one in which the camera moves right past Sam Neill and Laura Dern and straight up the neck of the brachiosaur. Then the brachiosaur bites some leaves off the trees forty feet above them and all these leaves and twigs come falling down. That was just an idea we got at the spur of the moment—and it's a great shot. Michael Lantieri wired clumps of branches to lean them over as if the brachiosaur was pulling down on the tree." Composited into the Hawaii background plate would be a full-motion CG brachiosaur. Most of the CG models were scratch built by hand in the computer. The CG team scanned in the T-rex and raptor model dinosaurs that had been designed and sculpted by the art department at Stan Winston Studio, and then—working with the basic data obtained from the scan—fleshed out the digital models with additional patch-meshes as needed.

In preparation for animating the completed brachiosaur, the CG animation team studied elephants, both on film and in person. "We went out to some wildlife parks," said Tippett, "so we could actually touch the elephants and feel their skin. We'd feel their muscles and get a sense of how they worked. Then we'd go back and apply that knowledge in our animation. In terms of movement, the brachiosaur was kind of a combination of an elephant and a giraffe—it had the long strides and grace of

To prepare for the animation task, ILM and Tippett animators studied and photographed real animals at Marine World and other wild animal parks.

CG lead supervisor Stefen Fangmeier works with senior animator Eric Armstrong on the animation of a CG dinosaur model.

the giraffe, but the weight and mass of the elephant."

The stampeding gallimimus herd, featured mid-way through the film, was another computer generated sequence. Background plates for the scene had originally been scheduled for the last day of shooting on Kauai—a plan that was scrapped when Hurricane Iniki came roaring through the island. A film crew later picked up the lost day's shooting over a hurried weekend on neighboring Oahu. "It had to be done fast," said Muren, "and we had trouble with the weather again. But it really turned out for the best because the location on Oahu was spectacular—much better than the one on Kauai. There were dramatic cliffs, with a narrow valley between them, whereas the other location had been an empty plain."

Animator Eric Armstrong had begun modeling a potential gallim-imus herd sequence at the earliest testing stage of ILM's involvement in *Jurassic Park*. Two test shots were made and the results were so amazing Spielberg wrote the sequence into the script. To emphasize the birdlike flocking of the gallimimuses—whose design had been based on the ostrich—Armstrong focused his animation on the movement of the herd as a whole, rather than on individual animals. "It is a point in the story that these animals were flocking together," noted Tippett, "and not just running around like a bunch of dimwitted reptiles. Since they were supposed to be precursors to birds, they would have had very sophisti-cated flocking mechanisms. So the way the herd moved as a group was very important. Individual animals were featured more once the stam-pede actually started. Eric had worked out a nice scenario where the parents kept the small gallis in the middle of the group as though they were protecting them. There were little details like that to enhance the scene subliminally."

Like the gallimimus, the velociraptors were slated to demonstrate the birdlike characteristics of the dinosaurs. Tippett had originally envisioned very hard, darting moves for the raptors; however, that concept changed as he observed the operation of Winston's full-size puppets on the set and as Spielberg expressed a preference for a more stealthy predator. "Spielberg thought that the quick, hard moves looked too much like stop-motion animation," Tippett explained. "We also had to concern ourselves with matching the full-size props, which didn't move in that quick way I had envisioned. So ultimately we moved away from the birdlike moves."

Spielberg's intention to reveal the animals in lingering shots present-

Clockwise: Randy Dutra, Craig Hayes and Tom St. Amand with the raptor DID puppet. / St. Amand animates the raptor DID. / Dutra with the T-rex DID.

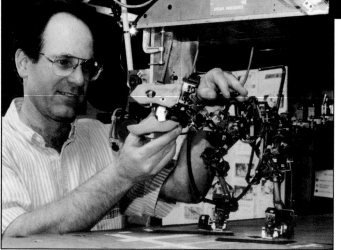

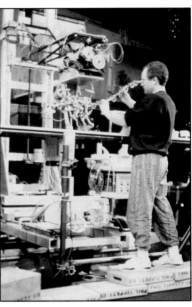

Right: Randy Dutra animates raptor DID
Left: Craig Hayes and Nick Blake with raptor DID and rig.

ed an additional challenge in animating the raptors. "We were going to see the behavior of these animals for extended lengths of time," Tippett commented. "But what were they going to be *doing* in all that time? It was fine if they had to perform a specific task, like jumping up on a table or walking from point A to point B. But when they were just standing there, it became a problem to fill the time with interesting action. One of the things I came up with was a flicking tongue movement. We shot all the animatics that way and it was a great time filler—the tongue movement would really enliven a dead scene. But when Jack Horner—the paleontologist on the show—saw it, he said: 'What are you doing? Raptors didn't do that! They physically couldn't do that! This is terrible!' We all wanted to be as authentic with these things as possible, so we got rid of the tongue movement."

Eager to explore the feasibility of producing computer generated dinosaurs, animator Steve Williams had made the modeling and animating of the T-rex a pet project when the film was still in the early stages of preproduction. Stefen Fangmeier then rendered the skin, lit it and composited the finished T-rex over a background photograph taken in an empty field near ILM. The result was spectacular. Previously convinced that his dinosaurs would have to be portrayed with a combination of Stan Winston's full-size mechanical puppets and go-motion techniques, Spielberg had enthusiastically opted for a CG alternative when presented with ILM's T-rex test.

Originally, the computer animated T-rex was to make its only appearance in the attack sequence, providing ambulatory full-body long shots that could not be achieved with Winston's animatronic creation. "In the main road attack, the CG reveals the full T-rex," said Muren, "and there are also shots where you see the T-rex close, such as knocking over the car—which is a very tight shot. We had originally been concerned about getting in too tight on these things, but we were eventually able to solve the aesthetic problems involved in that—problems like figuring out how light would react off the animal's skin as it was moving. That kind of artistic concern is very difficult to work out in CG because, really, the tools are not interactive. Another problem was making certain our stuff matched Stan's stuff—and it did. No one will ever see the difference, except maybe Stan. The lighting is slightly different on some of the shots, but even real actors in a film don't look exactly the same from shot to shot. So I think people will be convinced that it is all the same—and it is all real."

Encouraged by the CG team's progress, Spielberg eventually devised a new ending for the film in which computer generated raptors would be joined by the computer generated T-rex in a showdown between the fierce predators in the visitor center rotunda. Although the well-detailed computer models could have held up under close camera scrutiny, the director kept primarily to long shots for the sequence. "I felt that it was important to show the relative size and girth of the T-rex," Spielberg explained. "Unlike the main road attack, where I was trying to create a claustrophobic feeling, the ending in the rotunda seemed more impressive and more like a spectacle with the camera at a distance."

Computer graphics elements continued to be added to the film up until May 28. From his *Schindler's List* location in Poland, Spielberg maintained close contact with the CG effort through his production team at Amblin. "We would render shots to videotape to analyze the dinosaur movement, overall look and lighting," explained associate producer Colin Wilson. "Then we would send those videotapes to Steven for him to review. Once we got his approval, we would render the shots to film, then solicit his approval again for the final composite. We did that on a weekly basis for a while; and then, as it got closer to the end, there was more daily contact."

By the time they delivered their final shot, Industrial Light and Magic had been on *Jurassic Park* for well over two years. Though arduous and labor-intensive, it had proved to be one of the most exciting projects ever

Janet Healy, Dennis Muren and Phil Tippett discuss shots with Steven Spielberg via audiovisual satellite feed.

ILM animator James Strauss works on T-rex and raptor shots for the end rotunda sequence as George Murphy CG Supervisor works in background. All the dinosaur shots in the rotunda finale were computer generated.

taken on by the effects company; and as the film neared release, all of those involved in the effort buzzed with enthusiasm regarding the future applications of computer graphics in general—and the impact of *Jurassic Park* in particular. "*Jurassic Park* is going to be a mind-blowing experience," predicted Mark Dippe. "And it will be an important film in terms of filmmaking techniques. Dinosaur films have always been the classic effects films. A lot of effects techniques have been developed through the years in dinosaur movies—stop-motion, Claymation, men in rubber suits, cable-driven puppets, radio control puppets, go-motion . . . and now, full-motion computer animation. With *Jurassic Park*, we've created something that is in a direct line of the evolution of creature work."

Even Dennis Muren, a seasoned veteran who had approached the idea of creating dinosaurs through computer animation with caution, was pleasantly surprised at the extent to which the *Jurassic Park* work surpassed his own expectations. "When we first started on *Jurassic*, I didn't really expect the CG dinosaurs to be as spectacular as they are. I thought, 'Okay, our dinosaurs will be better than what we've seen in the past.' But these dinosaurs are absolutely unlike anything you've ever seen before—and I'm compelled by that."

Most likely, no one involved felt the impact of *Jurassic Park*'s achievement more profoundly than Phil Tippett. Tippett had begun the project with the intention of contributing his well-honed skills as a stop-motion

Lead ILM CG supervisor Stefen Fangmeier, ILM effects supervisor Dennis Muren and ILM CG artist Steven Rosenbaum discuss final lighting changes to raptor in the end raptor rotunda sequence.

animator, and had ended it with the conviction that *Jurassic Park* had marked a turning point in his career. "People have asked me, 'Where do you go from here?' I guess that depends on what kinds of movies are made in the future. At the moment, you've got to be a Steven Spielberg or a James Cameron to afford this kind of technology. So my hope is that there will still be productions that will use traditional stop-motion. It has been terrific to participate in this kind of cutting edge technology; but I also have concerns about it. For me, it was never that important to make things look real, which is pretty much the criterion for computer graphics; I always enjoyed the fact that the dinosaurs looked a little unreal. But the fact that we've gained another piece of equipment is great because it gives us more flexibility. When CG becomes more hands-on and comes down in price, then it will really be useful."

In a lush green valley just twenty minutes from Industrial Light and Magic lies Skywalker Ranch, a filmmaking complex built by George Lucas in the wake of his phenomenal success with *Star Wars* and its successors. Among the facilities housed there is Skywalker Sound, a company first established by Lucas to produce *Star Wars'* dynamic sound effects. Since then, Skywalker Sound had provided sound effects and mixing for films such as the *Indiana Jones* trilogy, *Terminator 2*, *Backdraft* and *JFK*, garnering many awards and much recognition in the process.

Because of its reputation within the industry, and its history with Steven Spielberg, Skywalker Sound was a prime candidate for the *Jurassic Park* sound assignment. It was an assignment that ranged from the unusual—such as producing all of the exotic sounds and vocalizations for the dinosaurs—to the more standard task of replacing lines of dialogue. Additionally, the sound facility would create sound effects not related to the dinosaurs, plus blend all the elements of the film's sound—including the musical score—into a satisfying final mix.

Heading the overall effort were sound designer Gary Rydstrom and supervising sound editor Richard Hymns. "My job started from the end of the picture editing period," explained Hymns. "I supervised all the sound editors for the different areas of the film—the sound effects editing, dialogue editing, dialogue replacement editing and so on." Working with Hymns were sound mix editor Gary Summers and sound designer Gary Rydstrom—both Academy Award recipients for *Terminator 2*.

Even in an age of audience sophistication, most moviegoers are unaware of the extent to which sound is recorded and mixed into a film long after principal photography has wrapped. "People go to the movies and they think that what they are hearing is what was recorded at the time," noted Hymns. "But there are many limitations in recording on a set. There is obviously the matter of safety, so recordings on the set tend to be on the wimpy side, particularly for explosions and crashes and things like that. To protect people, it's not feasible to use real glass or do real car crashes. So we replace all of that during the sound editing stage."

In addition to producing sound effects for action sequences, the sound editors also rerecorded dialogue that was inadequately recorded on the set. "We were lucky on *Jurassic Park* because the recordist did a very good job of recording the dialogue. We only had to replace about five hundred lines of dialogue, which wasn't much for this kind of film. On *Backdraft*, we replaced something like 2500 lines of dialogue because there was so much background noise from the fires on the set. Since *Jurassic Park* was shot on a sound stage, they were able to control the sound a lot more."

Recognizing the need for an exotic aural ambience, Hymns had traveled to the remote rain forests of Australia to gather unusual sounds shortly after securing the *Jurassic Park* contract in January 1992. "I recorded in Australia for two months," Hymns recalled. "We reasoned that it wasn't important to be literal with sounds from Costa Rica because this island was supposed to have foliage and animals that had been extinct for millions of years; so it made sense that there would be birds and insects that were from another age, as well. I was able to record a lot of strange stuff, unusual bird calls and night sounds to create moods that were eerie and scary—the kind of sounds you hear when you know something bad is about to happen."

More mundane sound effects were also required, such as the sound of the tour vehicles—which in the story were supposedly electromagnetically driven, but in reality were engine powered. "We had to remove the sound of the mechanical engines and replace it with the electric sound. I gathered a little library of electromagnetic car sounds to use for that. We also recorded jeeps running and coming to a stop, doors opening and closing, a lot of rain sounds—rain on canvas, rain on foliage. When we get a big film like this we like to go out and record all new stuff, even though we have a lot of these things already in our sound library. People in the business begin to recognize sounds that come from a particular studio or sound editing group. We try to change ours as much as possible so we don't get into a boring, repetitive gunshot sound or car crash sound. We like to keep everything as fresh as possible."

Perhaps the most creative aspect of the sound task was creating the various hoots, grunts, howls and screams of the dinosaurs. As with the visual representations of the dinosaurs, a sense of realism was essential in creating the dinosaur vocalizations. Spielberg encouraged Gary Rydstrom to manufacture a broad spectrum of sounds that would reveal the multifaceted natures of the animals. "In past dinosaur movies you would hear the same roar over and over again," Rydstrom noted. "What we wanted to do for *Jurassic* was develop a fuller, more natural vocabulary for these creatures—breathing and grunting and sniffing, even the sound of the eyelids moving or the nostrils flaring. We were striving to make it completely believable."

To prepare for the project, Rydstrom researched paleontological theories regarding dinosaur vocalizations. "I found out that there are many things scientists just don't know. For instance, with the brachiosaurs, it would make a tremendous difference in the way they sounded depending on whether their vocal box was located at the top of their necks or at the bottom of their necks. But paleontologists don't know *where* it was located. The input I got from Spielberg was just to make all the dinosaur sounds believably animalistic—something people could relate to. The line we had to walk was to come up with something that was new and different, yet also familiar enough so that people would believe these things actually exist. We couldn't get too far out with the dinosaur sounds—even if there was scientific evidence to support that—because the audience had to be able to connect with the animals."

Rydstrom recorded a variety of preliminary roars and other dinosaur sounds weeks before the start of filming in order to facilitate the puppeteering of the creatures on the set. "We looked at the videomatics and got a sense of how the dinosaurs were going to move and look; and we put sounds to those to see what worked. That way, when the animals were being puppeteered on the set, the operators had an idea of what the vocals would be like. They had to know how long the mouth would be open for a scream, what kind of pattern the screams had. For example, they came up with a throat movement for when the raptors make their gutteral clicking sounds. So the visual and vocal development of the dinosaurs went somewhat hand in hand."

Each of the dinosaur species featured in the film presented Rydstrom with a specific set of challenges. Among the most complex was the T-rex. "No single animal in the real world had a broad enough range of sounds to cover everything the T-rex needed to do," Rydstrom said. "So we used a combination of sounds from real animals to create the range of sounds

Below left: The sound editing crew at Skywalker Sound in San Rafael. *Below:* Sound designer Gary Rydstrom and supervising sound editor Richard Hymns.

for the T-rex. It was made up of elephant, alligator, penguin, tiger and dog sounds, all layered together. For the roar, we recorded a baby elephant that made a nice trumpet-like scream. We used that for the mid-range of frequencies, then added a tiger roar and an alligator growling sound. Alligators make this incredibly low, stuttering growl, which gave us the low frequency. The most enjoyable aspect of the T-rex was his breathing. I think we conveyed a far greater sense of his size with his breathing than we did with his roar. We recorded whale blowholes that I looped into a breathing rhythm to create those deep, resonant breaths."

Raptor sounds were also a combination of various real-life animal species. "The raptors had to sound as if they had intelligence—which, vocally, meant that they would make a greater variety of sounds, as if they had some ability to communicate with each other. We came up with a throaty clicking sound performed by a friend of mine. He was able to do this raspy click with his voice; and when we slowed it down, it was very interesting and guttural. We also recorded dolphins underwater at Marine World. Every once in a while they would make these really bizarre screams that were awful and high pitched, and those turned out to be the main element of the raptor attack screams. Another thing we recorded for the raptors was a goose hissing. We found these geese that were really nasty—and they not only hissed, they screamed. So for the scene where the two raptors are hunting Muldoon, we gave one raptor the goose scream and the other the dolphin scream, just to give them a separate identity. For their breathing, we recorded horses; and we found an African crane that made interesting calls to its mate that worked well for the raptors calling to one another."

A birdlike quality was also incorporated into the spitter vocalizations, with swan calls providing the primary hoots and howls—especially for the scene in which the small animal is assumed by Dennis Nedry to be harmless. When the tone of the scene changes—and the lethal nature of the spitter becomes apparent—the creature's vocal quality changes as well. "We used an egret, which has a very raspy call, for the spitter's attack mode. I also added my own voice, making a croaking sound, to give it some body and weight. For the cowl vibrating, we came up with a rattling sound that was actually a very exotic insect. The idea was to have these cute, high-pitched sounds at the beginning of the sequence, and then have them turn nasty and mean."

For the brachiosaurs, Rydstrom strayed from scientific evidence to better support Spielberg's vision of the elegant beasts. Conversations with paleontologists had revealed that brachiosaurs probably had extremely limited vocal capabilities. "Large animals, like giraffes, generally don't vocalize all that much. But the brachiosaurs in the movie convey a real sense of wonder and beauty, so we gave them a beautiful, melodic singing voice. We started with whale songs, because whales have a similar sense of size and grace. I also stretched out some donkey calls and echoed them to make them sound melodic. It was important that there be a pattern to the brachiosaur calls, as if one was calling and then there was an answer to it. The hardest thing about the brachiosaurs was that Grant imitates them in the movie. So we came up with the call first, and then we had to find somebody who could copy it."

Having made a vital contribution to the dinosaur characterizations, Gary Rydstrom was enthusiastic about his part in *Jurassic Park*. "*Jurassic Park* was a sound person's dream. In some ways it was a classic project, very much like doing a *King Kong* or any of the Ray Harryhausen films; in terms of sound, it followed a tradition. But it was very different from those previous films because it was much more realistic—it looked more believable and it had to sound more believable."

No less crucial to the film was the musical score. Traditionally, sound editors and composers have worked independently, with little or no contact until the final mixing stage. For *Jurassic Park*, however, the sound team broke with tradition and included composer John Williams in the process. "In the past," explained Richard Hymns, "the sound supervisor and the music composer went about their chores separately. The musician would be off writing somewhere and we would be working on our sound effects. Then we'd arrive at the mix together; and invariably there would be spots in the film where the sound effects and the score didn't mesh well. So we met with John earlier on, premixing our sound effects for the major scenes so that he would know what we were doing. That way we could avoid discordant things and we could also make 'holes' for each other so we wouldn't interfere with each other as much. It was a fairly new kind of collaboration, at least for me."

John Williams arrived at Skywalker Ranch at the end of February to begin composing music for the film. The arrangement was beneficial, not only because he would be in close proximity to the sound team, but also because it afforded the composer the opportunity to take advantage of the tranquil working environment the ranch offered. The best known and most venerated film composer of his time, Williams has scored more than seventy-five motion pictures in a career that has spanned four

Composer John Williams, another Spielberg collaborator, wrote the musical score for *Jurassic Park*.

decades. Considering his longtime association with Steven Spielberg, and their mutual respect for each other's work, his participation in the *Jurassic Park* project had been all but a given. "I have tremendous feeling for Steven," Williams averred. "We've been working colleagues for twenty years now; and in that time, my admiration for him as a person and as a filmmaker has grown. There is a kind of symbiosis between us, because of the films we have worked on together. Steven could have been a composer himself. He has that rhythmic sense in his whole being, and I think that is one of the great things about his directing—this rhythmic, kinetic sense he has. There is an ebb and flow of forces in the way he shoots a film."

Although Williams had been commissioned to write the *Jurassic Park* score early on, he had purposely removed himself from the project until it neared completion. "I generally find that it is better not to read the script. Reading a script and then seeing the film is rather like reading a novel and then seeing a film version of that novel—it never looks like you saw it in your mind's eye. So I prefer not to know what it is about, and just go into a darkened room and see the first cut and experience the film in terms of itself." Actual scoring of the film, with a full orchestra, would take place at the end of March, with Kathy Kennedy on hand to oversee the event in Spielberg's absence. Kennedy kept Spielberg in the loop by having each music cue transferred to digital audio tape and sent to the director daily for his approval.

With the music completed, all that remained for the sound crew was the final mix. Mixing is a process in which all the sound elements of a film—the dialogue, sound effects and music—are divided into individual tracks and them reassembled. "We will take the soundtrack," explained Richard Hymns, "which has the original dialogue on it, and split that up into half a dozen tracks or more, giving the mixer complete control over each line of dialogue. Then we do the same thing with the sound effects—we'll separate the wheels of the car from the engine of the car, the rain from the wind, the bird calls from the insect calls, and so on. So we wind up with as many as a hundred separate tracks. The mixer's job is to set the right volume for each individual track, then mix all of them smoothly down to about six tracks, which is the sound format in movie theaters."

By the end of April, all aspects of the sound editing were ready for Spielberg's final approval. For well over a year the sound editors at Skywalker Sound had been working on the project, and yet it was unlikely that anyone outside the business would be even remotely aware of their contribution to the film. "It is a somewhat thankless task," Hymns said philosophically. "If the audience notices our work, then we've spoiled the illusion; and if we do a really good job, nobody is aware of it."

Jurassic Park was completed by the end of May, well in time for its June 11 release. The premiere was much anticipated on many fronts: movie fans looked forward to it hungrily as the unofficial launching of the summer big-movie blitz; devotees of the novel were on hand to judge it against the delights of Crichton's original story; paleontology enthusiasts waited to see if, at long last, a definitive dinosaur movie had indeed been made; and Universal executives stood anxiously ready to measure its box office performance against other heavyweight seasonal contenders, such as Arnold Schwarzenegger's *The Last Action Hero.* Most significantly, however, Steven Spielberg, the production and design teams and the entire cast and crew anticipated the unveiling of *Jurassic Park* to that ultimate arbiter of every film's success or failure—the audience.

For key participants in the making of *Jurassic Park,* the hope of an enthusiastic response to the film was not motivated merely by a bottom-line mentality. Many had devoted three full years of their lives to the project; each had invested one hundred percent of their talents and energies. The challenges inherent in the project had demanded no less. "When we first read this book," said associate producer Lata Ryan, "all of us had the same thought: 'How in the world are we going to make this movie?' It was a huge, mind-boggling task, for *everyone.* Stan Winston had never had to create such enormous animatronic characters; Dennis Muren and the team at ILM had never produced the level of computer generated effects this film required; Phil Tippett had never had to do this kind of transitional work with computer graphics; Michael Lantieri had never had to devise rigs to interface with full-size dinosaurs; and Steven Spielberg had never required himself to bring in such a big movie so fast. Each of us had our own stake in *Jurassic Park,* our own personal challenge—and each of us, in our own way, rose to that challenge. We determinedly set out to figure out a way to bring this wonderful, huge, complicated book to the screen—and we did it."

PART FOUR

STORYBOARDS

Historians trace the evolution of storyboards to the Walt Disney Studio. There, in the early 1930s, when Disney was revolutionizing cartoon animation, studio artists would use rough sketches pinned onto bulletin boards to structure their storylines and establish a visual framework for each production prior to the commencement of animation. It was a convenient way to make certain that the multitudes of artists working on any given project shared a common vision.

For the same reason, storyboards became a vital component of special effects as technology blossomed and became increasingly more complex. Today many directors use them, not only for effects work, but also complex action sequences where visual references are useful in choreographing live-action photography. Some directors, Steven Spielberg included, have been known to storyboard their films from beginning to end.

For his adaptation of *Jurassic Park,* Spielberg employed storyboards in much the same manner as the early Disney animators—as a means of structuring his storyline and establishing visual framework. Under production designer Rick Carter, a team of artists—Ed Verreaux, Marty Kline, Tom Cranham, David Lowery, and John Bell—worked initially without a script, pulling favored sequences directly from the Michael Crichton source novel and translating them into visual images. Many of the concepts were taken directly from stick-figure sketches by the director. Over a period of months, even years, the storyboards were refined and revised, and even utilized by the screenwriters in developing the final shooting script.

What follows is a portfolio of these storybord sketches.

Main road attack

Ext. Park. Wide To Both Vehicles.

Int. Front Vehicle — Regis Shows Tim Goggles. Lex Sits In Backseat

Lex Looks Out Of Side Window.

Lex's P.O.V.: The Goat Teathered In The T-Rex Paddock.

Wide Over Lex To Regis. Tim Has Ducked Down Behind Seat. Then...

Tim Jumps Up Wearing Goggles ... "Boo."

Tim Climbs Into The Backseat With Lex. And....

Tim Leans On The Seat. Back, And Looks Toward Camera. The Camera Pushes In To....

A Close Shot Of Tim. He Adjusts The Focus On The Goggles

Tim's P.O.V.: Nightvision — He Twists And Adjusts The Goggles Until We Clearly See The Explorer With Grant And Genarro

THE SECOND EXPLORER: GRANT OPENS THE DOOR AND STICKS A BOTTLE OUT INTO THE RAIN

INT. VEHICLE 2. RAIN WATER FILLS THE BOTTLE.

WIDE TO GRANT & GENNARO....

GRANT LEANS BACK INTO THE VEHICLE AND TAKES A DRINK FROM THE BOTTLE.

BACK IN THE FRONT VEHICLE, LEX IS KICKING HER FEET AGAINST THE FRONT SEAT. BOOM. BOOM.... REGIS IS RESTING HIS EYES SHUT.

TIM TURNS "LISTEN DID YOU FEEL THAT." HE STOPS LEX'S KICKING LEGS. TIM JUMPS BACK INTO THE FRONT SEAT. PUSH IN TO CLOSE SHOT TIM.

TIM REMOVES THE GOGGLES. AND....

LOOKS DOWN TOWARD THE DASHBOARD.

WIDE OVER REGIS TO TWO GLASSES ON THE DASHBOARD. PUSH IN TOWARD GLASSES..

PUSH IN ON GLASS
VIBRATIONS START = DISAPPEAR =
START AGAIN
BOOM! BOOM...

THE WATER IN THE GLASS IS VIBRATING.

CLOSE ON REGIS CONTINUES TO REST THEM...

REGIS SUDDENLY OPENS HIS EYES.

CLOSE ON REGIS REFLECTION IN MIRROR. PUSH IN TO MIRROR. IT VIBRATES SECURITY PASS BOUNCES

PUSH IN CONTINUES INTO CLOSE SHOT REGIS'S FACE IN VIBRATING MIRROR.

REGIS MAYBE IT'S THE POWER TRYING TO
COME BACK ON!
TIM CLIMBS INTO THE BACK SEAT.

PUSH IN — TO TIM AS HE PUTS GOGGLES ON.

THEN TURNS TO LOOK OUTSIDE WINDOW.

PUSH IN...

NIGHTVISION P.O.V. THE CHAIN IS STILL THERE,
BUT THE GOAT IS GONE!

CLOSE TO LEX LOOKING AROUND...
O.S. — WE HEAR "BANG"!

LEX LOOKS UP TOWARD BUBBLE ROOF.

WIDE UP TO THE ROOF. A GOAT LEG LANDS ON
THE BUBBLE.

WIDE THRU THE MESHED FENCE TO TIM LOOKING OUT OF THE
SIDE WINDOW. CAMERA PUSHES IN

CONTINUE TO PUSH IN TO TIM

CLOSE SHOT TIM LOOKS OUT WINDOW.
CONTINUE RUSH. IN

PUSH-IN CONTINUES.
TIMS' MOUTH POPS OPEN.

TIMS' P.O.V THRU NIGHT VISION GLASSES
OF CLAW ON FENCE WIRES.

TIM LIFTS HIS GOGGLES OFF.

CLOSE ON CLAW. CAMERA PULLS BACK.

CAMERA CONTINUES TO PULL BACK
OVER TIMS' SHOULDER TO CLAW ON
FENCE. CAMERA PANS UP

TIGHT OVER TIM UP TO ROOF — REX AT FENCE GOAT HANGING OUT OF ITS MOUTH. THE REX SWALLOWS THE GOAT IN ONE BIG GULP.

GRANT TURNS — CAMERA PUSHES IN TO . . . .

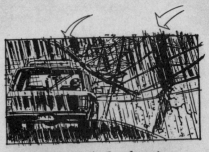

WIDE TO THE VEHICLE — THE FENCE CRASHES DOWN.

CLOSE ON REGIS. PANICS — RUNS TO DOOR

GENNARO LOOKING OUT WINDOW TO BUCKLING FENCE.

INT. VEHICLE — GENNARO TURNS LOOKS OUT WINDOW

REGIS OPENS DOOR AND RUNS.

TIM & LEX LOOK OUT WINDOW TOWARD FENCE

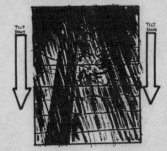

TILT DOWN   TILT DOWN

GENNARO'S P.O.V. CABLES POPS SNAP.

WIDE TO VEHICLES. REGIS RUNS PAST GRANT & GENNARO IN SECOND VEHICLE

OVER TIM & LEX AS THE FENCE IS PUSHED OVER. TILT UP! THE SIGN IS HAMMERED AGAINST THE DOME.

WIDE TO BOTH VEHICLES — THE T-REX TEARS ITS WAY THRU THE FENCE WIRES AND . . . .

INT. VEHICLE TO GRANT IN F.G & GENNARO . . . THEN . .

THE T. REX STEPS OVER THE BARRIER ONTO THE ROAD AND LOOKS DOWN AT BOTH VEHICLES

REX'S FOOT INTO FOREGROUND—

WIDE TO GRANT & GENNARO— GRANT PICKS UP RADIO.

GRANT & GENNARO TURN. LOOK OUT SIDE WINDOW CAMERA FOLLOWS. REX...

REX'S FEET TURN TOWARD SECOND VEHICLE

WIDE OVER GRANT & GENNARO TO T-REX LEGS CROSSING VEHICLE.. PAN WITH T-REXTO

T. REX MOVES PAST WINDOW. SEE REX EYE. GRANT LIFTS WALKIE TALKIE TO MOUTH "DON'T MOVE. DON'T MOVE."

INT. SECOND VEHICLE. GRANT & GENNARO REACT.

SIDE WINDOW OVER GRANT TO REX WALKING FOOT

INT. FRONT VEHICLE. LEX RUMMAGES AROUND TRYING TO FIND FLASHLIGHT

TIM REACHES ACROSS AND PULLS DOOR SHUT.   AND....

LEX FINDS FLASHLIGHT

TIGHT OVER TIM TOWARD THE REX. ENTERS LOOKS DOWN TOWARD TIM

WIDE OVER LEX WITH FLASHLIGHT TO TIM.

WIDE OVER GRANT & GENNARO. THE T-REX BENDS DOWN AND BUMPS THE WINDSHIELD... THEN

NOTICES THE LIGHT FLASHING AROUND IN THE FRONT VEHICLE. THE REX RAISES IT HEAD AND....

STRIDES TOWARD THE FRONT VEHICLE

INT. FRONT VEHICLE. TIM TURNS

TIM LUNGES AT LEX. TRIES TO GET FLASHLIGHT

LEX BACKS UP "NO IT'S MY FLASHLIGHT."

THE T-REX LOOKS DOWN IN THROUGH THE WINDSHIELD — CAMERA PANS WITH THE T-REX AS.....

IT MOVES PAST THE SIDE WINDOW. AND CONTINUES PAST.....

TIM WATCHES THE T-REX PASS BY...

LEX'S WINDOW. CLEARLY SEEING THE T-REX EYE

TIM TURNS AND REACTS TO THE T-REX

T-REX LIFTS HER HEAD UP OUT OF FRAME

CAMERA CRANES UP TO......

CONTINUES CRANE UP....

OVER T-REX DOWN TO TIM & LEX.

LOW OVER TIM & LEX UP TO THE T-REX ... IT ...

DOWN ANGLE: FLASHLIGHT FLARES INTO CAMERA AS LEX LOOKS UP AND SCREAMS

HITS THE BUBBLE ROOF KNOCKING IT DOWN INTO THE VEHICLE.

THE BUBBLE FALLS DOWN ONTO TIM & LEX.

OVER TIM & LEX TO THE T-REX LUNGING DOWN

SIDE ANGLE TO TIM & LEX. THE REX CONTINUES TO PUSH DOWN.

TURNS DOWN TOWARD THEM.

TIGHT OVER THE T-REX DOWN TO TIM & LEX.

THE T-REX RUSHES DOWN - TIM RITE HIS FEET UP AGAINST THE BUBBLE, AND ....

THE REX PUSHES THE BUBBLE DOWN FURTHER, TRAPPING TIM & LEX.

TIM'S P.O.V. THRU HIS LEGS TO THE T-REX

GRANT REACTS.

ANGLE PAST T-REX LEG... THE KIDS WATCH IN HORROR

DOLLY AROUND BEHIND T-REX LEG.

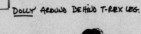

...DOLLY INTO ANGLE THRU T-REX LEGS... SHE ROARS AND...

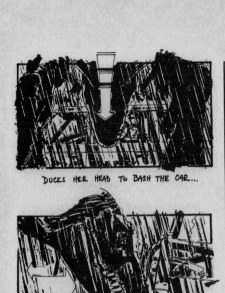

DUCKS HER HEAD TO BASH THE CAR...

T.REX BASHES HER SNOUT INTO THE SIDE OF THE EXPLORER.

REX STARTS TO TIP THE EXPLORER OVER.

AS KIDS FALL INTO CAMERA, THE GLASS SHATTERS, SHARDS FLYING EVERY WHERE.

THE T-REX HITS THE SIDE OF THE EXPLORER . . . .

IT FLIPS AND . . .

INT. VEHICLE. TIM & LEX TUMBLE AROUND..

THRU THE FENCE WIRES THE T-REX STARTS TO NUDGE THE EXPLORER UP THE BARRIER

THE REX 'ROARS'

WIDE TO THE T-REX STEPS ON VEHICLE CHASSIS AND

THE FORCE OF THE T-REX STEP CAUSES THE REAR WINDOW TO SHATTER.. AND THEN

THE T-REX LEANS OVER AND RIPS THE REAR AXLE AND . . .

PULLS THE GUTS OUT OF THE UNDER-CARRIAGE. THEN . . .

STRIKES A SECOND TIME...

GRANT REACTS.

TIM & LEX CRAWL FORWARD. THROUGH THE MUD AND WATER

GENARRO REACTS

THE T.REX LEANS OVER TOWARD THE FRONT OF THE VEHICLE AND..

CLOSE ON THE T.REX CHEWING ON THE TIRE
CAMERA CRANES DOWN TO.

COLLAPSE DOWN.

A SEAT COMES DOWN AND PINS TIM IN THE MUD

CONTINUE CRANE DOWN TO

THE EXPLORER CRUSHES DOWN MUD AND RAIN WATER POUR IN.

T-REX BACKING UP, DRAGGING THE EXPLORER, SWINGING IT LEFT AND RIGHT.

TO TIM & LEX. TRAPPED INSIDE.

DOLLY BACK: *TIM* AND *LEX* TURN AND SCRAMBLE AS THE MUD RISES (FROM THE REX PUSHING DOWN ON THE CAR.

...AND DRAGS THE HEADLIGHT RIGHT INTO CAMERA

WIDE TO GRANT. JUMPS OUT OF THE VEHICLE. AND....

WALKS FORWARD. SETS OFF A FLARE AND WAVES IT TOWARD THE T-REX.

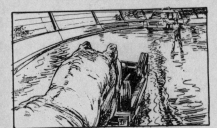

CRANE UP. AS THE T-REX REACTS & WE SEE THE GLEAM OF THE FLARE.

WIDE OVER GRANT TO THE T-REX. GRANT GETS THE T-REX ATTENTION - THEN....

OVER THE T-REX TO GRANT. HE THROWS THE FLARE AND...

THE T-REX TURNS.... ANY....

WIDE TO THE T-REX LUNGING TOWARD THE FLARE

GENNARO: TERRORIZED - LEAPS OUT OF THE CAR.

AND MAKES A RUN FOR HIS LIFE

MALCOLM RUNS. THE T-REX TURNS SEEING MALCOLM. AND...

CAMERA DOLLYS BACK WITH MALCOLM.

TAKES PURSUIT. KNOCKING GRANT OUT OF THE WAY CAMERA CONTINUES TO PULL BACK

STEADICAM BACK WITH MALCOLM - DROP INTO LOW - UP - ANGLE WITH T-REX IN PURSUIT. (RESTROOM SIGN WHIPS THRU FRAME AS WE RUN)

Dolly Back into Bathroom..

cont'd.. T-Rex pushes Malcolm thru door!..

cont'd.. Malcolm lies unconscious, in mid-ground the last wall falls, revealing,...

cont'd.. T-Rex upon Malcolm...

cont'd... T-Rex pushing Malcolm forward, trying to bite him, & collapsing building...

cont'd... Gennaro revealed sitting on commode!..

INT. restroom... Gennaro hides in stall, locks door...

ROOM SHAKING

UPSHOT on roof collapsing into CAM.

cont'd... Rex leg into sc., Gennaro reacts!..

cont'd... ROOM SHAKING

cont'd... UPSHOT roof collapses into CAM wipes scene....

(closer) Gennaro screams (Rex jaws in F.G.)

We hear T-Rex pounding closer... ROOM SHAKING

Malcolm becomes buried under restroom debris...

GRANT RUSHES TO THE VEHICLE TO SEE IF
THE KIDS ARE HURT.

CAMERA PUSHES IN TO

GRANT LEANING IN TO KIDS

INT. VEHICLE. LEX "DR. GRANT".

GRANT PULLS LEX OUT OF THE VEHICLE. PUSH. IN
TO GRANT & LEX.... "TIM'S UNCONCIOUS, HE
WON'T MOVE."

GRANT "LEX, LEX, ARE YOU OKAY!"

LEX SCREAMS. GRANT TURNS TO SEE...

GRANT COVERS LEX MOUTH.

GRANT "HE CAN'T SEE US IF WE DON'T MOVE—
...DON'T MAKE A SOUND."

THEY STARE

OUT OVER CAMERA... AND...

GRANT COVERS LEX'S MOUTH AS A BIG REX
FOOT LANDS IN THE FOREGROUND.

OVER GRANT & LEX.. THE REX LEANS IN AND SNIFFS
THE VEHICLE.

THE REX SWINGS HER HEAD UP NEAR GRANT & LEX—
AND WITH A HUGE SNORT BLOWS GRANT'S HAT OFF

...THE REX PULLS BACK, OUT OF FRAME.

THE T. REX LOWERS DOWN. LOOKING FOR SIGNS OF LIFE...
GRANT & LEX ARE MOTIONLESS...

THE REX. BUTTS THE EXPLORER. WITH IT'S SNOUT—
GRANT & LEX TUMBLE WITH THE VEHICLE

BEHIND T-REX FEET AS THE CAR SPINS. GRANT AND LEX SCRAMBLE TO KEEP AHEAD OF THE CAR...
PUSH IN — BETWEEN T-REX LEGS

PUSH THRU T-REX LEGS AS GRANT & LEX SCRAMBLE...

PUSH IN AS RED TAIL LIGHT WIPES ACROSS FRAME...

GRANT & LEX ROLL (& DROP OUT OF FRAME) CAMERA DOLLY ACROSS TO FOLLOW ACTORS...

"ACTORS" SIT UP INTO FRAME   CAR SPINS TO A STOP

DOLLY WITH CAR INTO LOW-UP-ANGLE OVER GRANT & LEX TO T-REX

INSIDE EXPLORER. TIM AWAKENS AND SCREAMS!

T-REX LOOMS OVER GRANT AND LEX

CRANE DOWN...

CRANE DOWN

CRANE DOWN WITH T-REX HEAD AS IT LOWERS TO LOOK INTO THE CAR FOR TIM.

INT. VEHICLE. TIM TRIES TO UNWEDGE HIMSELF..

ANGLE OVER TIM, INSIDE THE EXPLORER. THE REX PUSHES THE CAR WITH IT'S SNOUT — PUSHING UP A WAVE OF MUD...

THE T-REX. WITH A MOUTHFUL OF MUD. LOOKS IN AT TIM.

THE T'REX PUSHES THE VEHICLE TOWARD THE MOAT

Grant grabs a fallen cable. As He & Lex make it over the wall.

Wider. Grant & Lex slide down cable....

... Into The F.G. As The Vehicle Begins To Be Pushed Over The Border Toward Them.

Up Angle. Lex is unaware that she is choking Grant.

Grant & Lex swing across and....

Does Not Make it Across To The Cables...

Grant & Lex Look Up To See

NEDRY ENCOUNTERS THE SPITTER

Nedry drives along rainy, slick road.

close on Nedry at the wheel.

NEDRY'S P.O.V.

Nedry reacts & swerves —

Nedry puts Rover into a swerving skid...

(cont'd) Rover skids hi-speed thru fence

Nedry's Rover goes down culvert into a raging gulley

C/u Nedry looks at stuck Rover

...as wheels spin & spray. Rover hopelessly stuck.

Nedry gets out of Rover, look around for a path...

PAN-PAN! Nedry sees a lower access road thru park...

\TILT-UP \ from flooded road to Nedry above

Nedry grabs winch & heads for a secure tree...

He hears 'hooting' getting closer & louder

PUSH-IN to meet Nedry walking fwd. w/ cable...

cont'd... PUSH-IN to meet Nedry walking to tree w/ cable...

cont'd... PUSH-IN to meet Nedry trudging fwd...

cont'd... PUSH-IN meet Nedry reaching tree...

PAN...

Spitter leaps walk into F.G... Nedry in B.G. hears splash!...

cont'd... Nedry whirls around @ splashing sound ... Spitter continues hopping thru scene...

Med. C/U - Nedry snugs cable around tree...

Nedry stands & is surprised by :HOOT:

cont'd... PULL-BACK w/Nedry as Spitter pokes at again :HOOT!

cont'd... Spitter darts back in bushes PULLBACK w/Nedry running toward camera

Nedry slugging thru scene, hand-over-hand along winch line...

CRANE-UP from LOW ANGLE Nedry as he trudges hand-over-hand to...

Nedry gestures "Get outta' here!"; Spitter looks at his hand stupidly...

cont'd... Nedry turns & continues slogging towards his Jeep...

cont'd... to CRANE-UP ends... in HIGH angle down reveal Spitter behind Nedry - it takes a playful hop following him...

cont'd... Spitter looks quizzically @ Nedry "?!"...

extreme wide shot as Nedry trudges on... spitter continues hopping.

cont'd... Nedry turns to face the little spitter it playfully leaps again towards him!

cont'd... Nedry shouts & gestures again "GO ON - GET!" Spitter again follows his gesture obediently...

LOW ANGLE on Nedry slogging hand over hand... spitter behind him

(reverse past Spitter) it - HOOTS!

cont'd...Spitter looks at Nedry dully... "?"

cont'd... Spitter hops once again after Nedry... he turns...

Nedry mutters "Jeez... stupid lizard..."

Nedry picks up a stick, thinking the Spitter wants to play... "Here boy!..."

cont'd... Nedry throws stick over Spitter, hoping to distract him "... GO FETCH!".

Stick thrown over Spitter, sails over his head, Spitter "doesn't get it"

cont'd... Spitter turns to watch stick splash behind him..

cont'd... Spitter looks quizzically @ Nedry "?"

cont'd... Spitter cocks it's head, says "HOOT!"

Nedry now totally annoyed "Aww, no wonder you're extinct!"...

cont'd... Nedry turns to climb slope, slowly pulls himself against the current..

WIDE TO NEDRY PULLING HIMSELF UP CABLE.

Spitter approaches on embankment...

cont'd: Spitter raises up; Nedry tries backing up...

(rev?x) over spitters collar/hood - Nedry reads

Ol' Spitter readies to spit...

(mid) Nedry scrambles over gulley - Spitter in pursuit.

Nedry over top open rover door

Nedry readies to climb into rover - glances back to pursuer...

cont'd ... Nedry gets direct hit by Spitter!

closer on Nedry PUSH IN as he blindly looks back...

We hear more than we see, the Spitter
"hits" Nedry - he screams desperately
and his counterfeit shaving cream can
flies out the window!

Nedry struggles blindly, jumps forward to get into Rover...

NEDRY LOOKS BACK, BUT THERE'S NO SPITTER

the shaving cream can hits the mud - :GLup! -
we hear blood curdling scream OS.!

cont'd ... Nedry butts head on door frame ..

WIDE OVER NEDRY TO THE SPITTER it...

cont'd ... a wave of mud & rain slops over
the shaving can... we hear Nedry's
final scream/gurgle-gasp. etc...

cont'd ... Nedry staggers back in severe distress ...

LOOKS TOWARD THE PASSENGER SEAT.

Nedry stands and turns to track, trying to get away...

ESCAPE FROM THE T-REX

THEY HEAR SOMETHING OFF-CAMERA....

ELLIE & MULDOON LOOK BACK....

MALCOLM POPS UP IN THE FOREGROUND

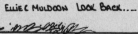

SUDDENLY.. THE T.REX BURSTS THROUGH THE JUNGLE....

ELLIE THUMBLES FOR THE IGNITION KEY. TURNS THE KEY.. SLAMS THE JEEP INTO GEAR.

CLOSE ON ELLIE RELEASING THE CLUTCH AND HITTING THE GAS PEDAL....

LOW ANGLE TO THE JEEP_ THE WHEELS SPIN THE JEEP TAKES OFF_

THE JEEP SPEEDS AWAY_

OVER MALCOLM IN THE F.G TO THE T-REX CLOSING IN.

CLOSE ON ELLIE LOOKS DOWN AND SEES.....

OBJECTS ARE CLOSER THAN THEY APPEAR

THE T-REX IN SIDE MIRROR....

Rack Focus On The T-Rex

Low Wide Tracking With Vehicle As...

Malcolm Falls Forward And Knocks The Gear Lever Out Of Gear,

Wide To The Group... Looking Toward Camera. A Fallen Tree Blocks Their Path Ahead...

The T-Rex Plows Thru Tree In Front Of Jeep...

Ellie Grabs The Gear Lever And...

They look forward...

They All Turn To The Front And....

Camera Moves Closer To Jeep. The T-Rex Closes In And....

Slams The Jeep Back Into Gear.

Duck . Just As The Windshield Hits The Tree... And...

Rams The Side Of The Jeep....

Close On Ellie's Foot On The Gas Pedal

Shatters Into Camera...

Inside. Everyone Feels The Impact.

Over Malcolm To The T-Rex Close To The Jeep...

THE JEEP PICKS UP SPEED... THE T-REX
STARTS TO FALL BACK....

FURTHER AND FURTHER....

CLOSE ON GROUP LOOKING RELEAVED!...

THE JEEP DRIVES AWAY...

INTO THE DISTANCE....

FENCES
AND FEAR

EXT. VISITOR CENTER - MULDOON & ARNOLD WALK DOWN STEPS INTO 2 SHOT

STRAIGHT MOVING P.O.V.

PAN WITH MULDOON & ARNOLD ALONG PATH... TO....

A HUGE HOLE IN THE RAPTOR PEN FENCE

OVER MULDOON & ARNOLD TO THE RAPTOR PEN... AWAY....

MULDOON TURNS TOWARD CAMERA, AND TILT DOWN TO....

TO MULDOON.... PAN DOWN MULDOON'S BODY TO

MULDOON'S FEET. _CAMERA PULLS BACK_ REVEALING RAPTOR FOOT PRINTS. CONTINUE THE.....

CAMERA PULL BACK. TO A WIDE ANGLE SHOT OF MULDOON & ARNOLD. RAPTOR FOOTPRINTS LEAD OFF INTO ALL DIRECTIONS. _CAMERA CONTINUES PULL BACK_

PULL BACK THROUGH F.G. JUNGLE TO MULDOON & ARNOLD IN DISTANCE. THE FOOTPRINTS LEAD OFF INTO THE JUNGLE.

NICE HIGH ANGLE DOWN TO MULDOON & ARNOLD. ARNOLD DECIDES TO GO TO THE MAINTENANCE SHED AND MULDOON STARTS BACK TO THE VISITOR CENTER TO WARN GROUP. _CAMERA PULLS BACK & CRANES DOWN_. WITH.....

MULDOON WALKING BACK. _CONTINUE CRANE DOWN & MOVE BACK WITH MULDOON_ TO....

TRACK BACK WITH MULDOON. IN THE DISTANCE ARNOLD PROCEEDS TO THE MAINTENANCE SHED.

WIDE OVER THE GROUP TO MULDOON WALKING TOWARD THEM....

MULDOON WALKS UP THE STEPS TO GROUP....

WIDE OVER MULDOON TO GROUP. GROUP PICK UP GENNARO.... AND....

WALK DOWN THE STEPS....

LOW WIDE ANGLE TO GROUP ALONG PATH TOWARD HAMMOND'S COMPOUND.

CRANE DOWN WITH GROUP ALONG PATH... AND...

REVEAL COMPOUND FENCE IN F.G. — CONTINUE. TO...

INT. HAMMOND'S QUARTERS - DOORS FLY OPEN AND THE GROUP ENTER.

THE FENCE AROUND THE COMPOUND...

CRANE DOWN. THRU GATES AS GROUP WALK THRU GATES INTO COMPOUND...

OVER HAMMOND, AS THEY LAY GENNARO ON THE COUCH, MULDOON SCOUTS THE HOUSE.

DOLLY BACK — GRANT & KIDS COME OUT OF FOREST AND RUN TOWARD THE FENCE... AND...

CAMERA CRANES DOWN OVER ELLIE &...

CAMERA RUSHES IN ON HAMMOND AS HE TURNS "ARNOLD"

PULL BACK THRU THE FENCE AS WIRES WIPE INTO FRAME. THE...

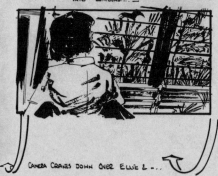

CONTINUE PUSH-IN "WHERE'S THE POWER!"

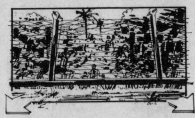

CAMERA CONTINUES TO PULL BACK TO WIDE SHOT. "GRANT "WE'LL HAVE TO CLIMB OVER IT!"

TILTS UP OVER ELLIE'S BACK TO THE FENCE...

MOVING P.O.V THRU HEAVY JUNGLE.... JUNGLE CLEARS TO REVEAL

HIGH ANGLE DOWN PAST F.G FENCE LIGHT. TO GRANT & KIDS. THEY SEE THAT THE POWER IS OFF... "THAT'S A BIG CLIMB CAN YOU HANDLE IT LEX!"

HIGH ANGLE DOWN TO GROUP- CLOSING GATE --- SEE THE MOAT ON OTHER SIDE OF THE FENCE.

CLOSE-UP
-LACING UP A
PUMP RUNNING SHOE

LOW ANGLE - THE GROUP WATCHES AS ELLIE LACES
UP HER RUNNING SHOES & PUMPS THEM - SSST, SSST

ELLIE WALKS OUT THE GATE OF HAMMOND'S LODGE

ELLIE WALKS OUT OF THE GATE.

HIGH WIDE ANGLE DOWN - TO ELLIE ALONG PATH.

LOW ANGLE ON THE BACK OF ELLIE'S SHOES TOWARD
THE MAINTENANCE SHED.

CLOSE ON ELLIE. SHE HEARS SOMETHING!

BACK AT HAMMOND'S QUARTERS - MULDOON HOLDS HIS
HAT AS THE WIND PICKS UP.

OVER ELLIE THE WIND PICKS UP BLOWING LEAVES
EVERYWHERE AND...

ELLIE TURNS. SPOOKED - SHE TURNS BACK AND...

SPRINTS TOWARD CAMERA. DOLLY BACK WITH ELLIE
AND PAN WITH

PAN WITH ELLIE

PAN WITH ELLIE AS SHE RUNS....

ALONG PATH TOWARD MAINTENANCE SHED.

BACK AT THE COMPOUND... PUSH-IN TO WU GIVING ELLIE
DIRECTIONS.

EXT. PARK FENCE... A HAND ENTERS AND GRABS
ONE OF THE TENSION WIRES. THEN...

A SECOND HAND ENTERS, AND GRABS A LOWER WIRE... THEN

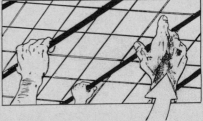

A THIRD HAND ENTERS IN THE F.G AND...

TIM PULLS HIMSELF UP INTO FRAME...

LOW WIDE ANGLE UP TO GRANT, TIM & LEX CLIMBING...

HIGH ANGLE DOWN TO TIM, GRANT & LEX ON FENCE.

WIDE LOW ANGLE UP TO ELLIE ENTERING THE MAINTENANCE SHED.

CLOSER TO ELLIE. SHE TURNS PALM TOWARDS HER. AND...

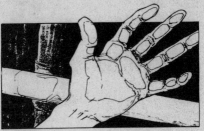

ELLIE'S P.O.V. OF HER HAND COVERED IN PAINT.

ELLIE CONTINUES INTO SHED

WIDE OVER ELLIE IN F.G TO SIGN ON WALL...

CAUTION! SPRAY PAINTING QUIDADO! ESTAMOS PINTANDO ESTA MOJADO

WIDE TO ELLIE AT DOORWAY. SHE MAKES HER WAY DOWN THE STAIRWELL AND... CAMERA DOLLIES WITH...

ELLIE INTO LOW WIDE ANGLE UP TO ELLIE... AND DOLLY AROUND.

LOW ANGLE DOLLY UP TO...

C.U. OF ELLIE'S FACE BOTTOM LIT BY FLASHLIGHT.

LOW WIDE ANGLE UP TO GRANT, TIM & LEX AT TOP OF FENCE.

HIGH ANGLE DOWN TO FENCE.

INT. MAINTENANCE SHED... ELLIE'S TRACKING P.O.V.

TRACKING BACK WITH ELLIE ALONG CORRIDOR

WIDE TOWARD ELLIE, SHE SHINES FLASHLIGHT ONTO POWER BOX....

ELLIE WALKS TO BOX AND...

OVER ELLIE TO POWER BOX. SHE FLIPS COVER OPEN THEN...

A PANEL OF SWITCHES IS REVEALED.

AT THE FENCE
WIDE TO GROUP. CRANE DOWN

BACK AT THE POWER BOX - ELLIE FLIPS THE SAFETY CAPS OFF.

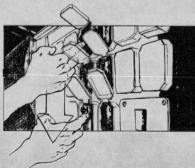

PAN DOWN WITH ELLIE. FLICKING SWITCHES ON!

ELLIE STEPS BACK. WAITS FOR INSTRUCTIONS.

PUSH-IN TO

OVER THE RADIO "FLIP SWITCHES 4·5·6·8 BEFORE YOU ENGAGE MAIN POWER."

ELLIE TURNING SWITCHES ON IN SEQUENCE.

CLOSE ON ELLIE'S FINGER ACTIVATING GENERATOR POWER.

EXT. PARK FENCE - BLUE LIGHT STARTS TO FLASH 'ON'.

EXT. FENCE. HIGH ANGLE DOWN TO GRANT AND...

LOOKS UP TOWARD CAMERA. TOWARD LIGHT.

AT THE FENCE. GRANT TRIES TO PERSUADE TIM TO JUMP.

ELLIE'S HAND IS GETTING CLOSER TO THE SWITCH.

LETS GO OF WIRE AND JUMPS DOWN.

HIGH ANGLE DOWN TO GRANT & LEX.

CLOSE ON LEX LOOKING AT TIM.

WIDE ANGLE TO LEX JUMPING DOWN. GRANT CATCHES HER.

BACK IN THE MAINTENANCE SHED. ELLIE REACHES TOWARD POWER "SWITCH".

CLOSE ON TIM   HE...

HIGH ANGLE DOWN. TIM WON'T LET GO HE'S FROZEN.

CLOSE ON GRANT. YELLING UP AT TIM.

TURNS TO LOOK DOWN.

BACK IN THE MAINTENANCE SHED. ELLIE IS LOOKING INSIDE THE MAIN POWER BOX.

LOW ANGLE UP TO TIM.

CLOSE ON ELLIE'S HAND AROUND HANDLE OF SWITCH.

CLOSE ON TIM'S HANDS. HE...

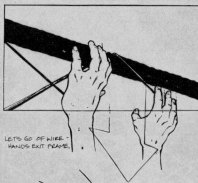

LET'S GO OF WIRE - HANDS EXIT FRAME.

POWER SWITCH "ON".

THE FENCE STROBE FLASHES.

WIDE TO TIM FALLING. GRANT....

CATCHES TIM. THEY BOTH FALL BACK...

GRANT AND TIM FALL BACK AS- BRANCHES MAKE CONTACT WITH FENCE. IT SPARKS!

Ellie flips on light switches - row of overhead lights come on in B.G....

Ellie turns toward lights...

...cont'd... row of overhead lights come on in sequence towards Ellie.

Ellie watches with some relief - lights come on overhead...

cont'd... light comes on behind Ellie...

cont'd... Raptor lurches at Ellie, nearby light explodes - sparks fly - Raptor wedged in pipes...

Raptor reaches out snapping @ Ellie...

cont'd ... Raptor snaps & strains to reach Ellie...

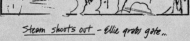

Steam shoots out - Ellie grabs gate...

cont'd... Ellie slams gate on Raptor...

Ellie staggers back in shock!...

cont'd... a disembodied arm plops onto her shoulder...

cont'd... Ellie shakes arm off & trips on...

Ellie's PDV ... Arnold's legs that she tripped on...

Ellie dashes off... with a last look @ Raptor.

TILT DWN. w/ Raptor clearing thru chain link...

O.T.S. Ellie heads for daylight...

PULLBACK w/ Ellie running forward...
we hear Raptor's ferocious roar echo thru bldg!...

cont'd... PULLBACK Ellie reaches the light...

She bolts up the stairs...

Raptor into sc.

cont'd... Raptor jumps into frame...

Ellie clears the door & slams it on the nearby Raptor's roar!

cont'd... she rests a beat Raptor head muffled sounds thru door...

RAPTORS STALK TIM AND LEX

INTERIOR: VISITOR'S CENTER — WIDE, HIGH ANGLE....
— GRANT ENTERS WITH LEX & TIM.

GRANT LEAVES TIM & LEX, GOES TO FIND GROUP.

HIGH WIDE SHOT — TRACKING AS THEY WALK;
TO REVEAL THE SKELETON SCULPTURE.

GRANT LEAVES, STEVE (COOK) TAKES TIM & LEX TO
FOOD COUNTER.

REVERSE HIGH ANGLE — GRANT AND KIDS PASS THRU
SKELETAL DISPLAY TOWARD CAFETERIA.

TIM AND LEX GRAB DRINKS AND...

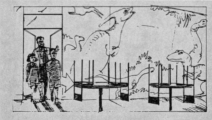

GRANT TIM AND LEX ENTER CAFETERIA.

WALK TOWARD TABLE..., STEVE ENTERS
KITCHEN.

SITS IN F.G. LEX GRABS STRAW

TURNS BACK TOWARD LEX...

TIM AND LEX LOOK AROUND

WIDE OVER TIM TO LEX

AND STARTS TO MOVE...

WIDE HIGH ANGLE DOWN TO TIM AND LEX

CLOSE OVER TIM TO LEX. SHE SPOTS SOMETHING

LEX RUNS TOWARD KITCHEN DOOR.

TIM AT LIGHT SWITCH. FLIPS EVERY SWITCH NOTHING!

IN THE B.G. WE SEE THE RAPTOR ON THE MURAL MOVING TIM...

LEX BURSTS THRU DOOR INTO KITCHEN –

TIM & LEX RUN DOWN AISLE. CAMERA RUNS BACK THEY...

TURNS LOOKS AT RAPTOR AND...

TIM FOLLOWS.

HIDE AT END OF AISLE BEHIND COUNTER... THE RAPTOR APPEARS.

RAPTOR'S P.O.V OF
PART OF TIM HIDING BEHIND THE COUNTER.

THE RAPTOR OPENS THE DOOR.

SNIFF·· SNIFF·· SNIFF·· SNIFF··

OVER TIM & LEX TO THE DOOR BEING HIT REPEATEDLY···
BAM! BAM! BAM!

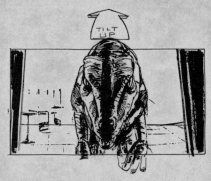

AND RISES· LOOKING AROUND·

WIDE ANGLE TO TIM & LEX· THE RAPTOR SNIFFS AT
THE BOTTOM OF THE DOOR·

RAPTOR'S P.O.V OF THE DOOR HANDLE·

RAPTOR TRIES TO LOOK THRU THE STEAMED GLASS·
THEN····

CLOSE ON TIM & LEX. TRACK-IN

BEAUTY SHOT OF THE RAPTOR
BACK LIT IN DOORWAY·

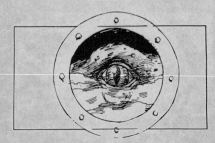

THE STEAM VANISHES· THE RAPTOR LOOKS·
AND ·SEES·

CLOSE ON THE DOOR HANDLE STARTS TO TURN—

THE RAPTOR ENTERS· TIM & LEX WATCH·

LOW ANGLE UP TO THE SECOND RAPTOR
ENTERING.

THE RAPTORS TURN AND VOCALIZE. TO EACH
OTHER

WIDE ANGLE THE RAPTORS SPLIT.

start.. TRACKING W/ kids...

CAMERA TRACKING   cont'd
DOLLY WITH TIM & LEX AS THEY CRAWL ABOVE THE RAPTOR
STALKS.

low angle TRACKING
We hear the Raptor's claws 'click-clacking' on tile
PAN w/ to kid's hands 'pitter-patter' on floor.

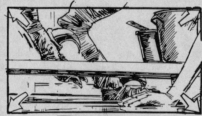

cont'd.. PULLBACK ends.. low-angle shot
contrasting claws & hands.

cont'd... PULLBACK ends wide as Tim & Lex crss by Raptors.

cont'd .. Raptor's looking for kids swings tail knocking
pots and pans onto kids.

PULLBACK cont'd kids round bend..
they scramble very fast
to hide ..

cont'd. PAN kids around corner... Raptor starts to
poke head thru counter

cont'd. PAN cont'd w/ kids around corner, Raptor cranes neck
out thru counter just as they
are out-of-view...

cont'd .. PAN ends w/ kids huddled behind counter-end...
Tim bangs into hanging utensils...

Raptors 1 & 2 respond to 'spoon' noise...

Spoon spins to a stop...

cont'd... Raptors respond to noise...

cont'd... Lex rounds far corner... Raptors head towards Tim...

cont'd... Raptors head towards Tim...
Lex peer around corner

cont'd... w/ Raptors they turn towards noise...

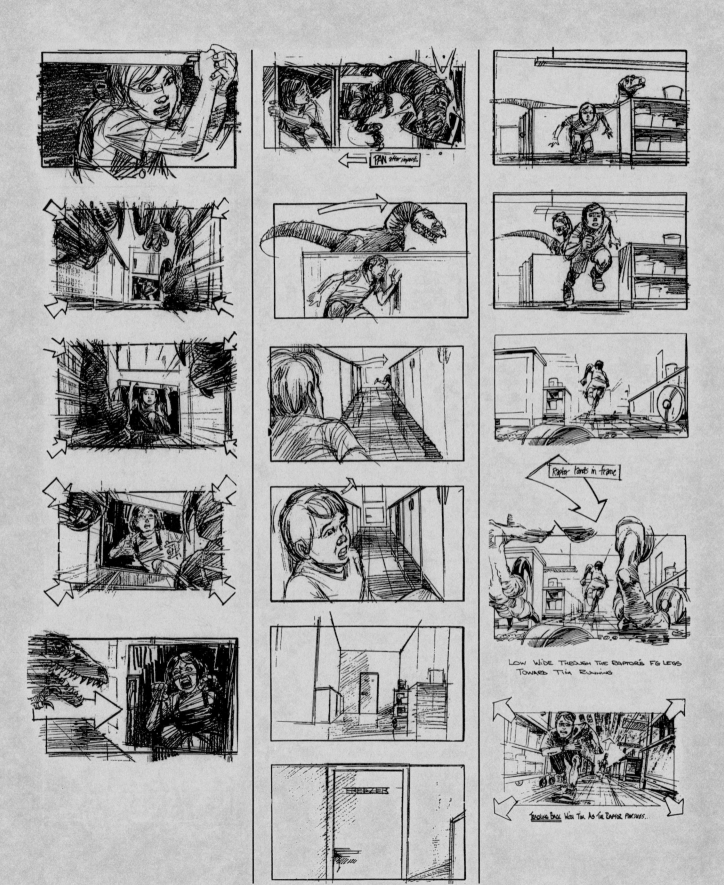

PAN after impact

Raptor lands in frame

LOW WIDE THROUGH THE RAPTOR'S FG LEGS
TOWARD TIM RUNNING

TRACKING BACK WITH TIM AS THE RAPTOR PURSUES...

TRACKING BEHIND THE RAPTOR'S FEET TO TIM. THE MOMENTUM OF DOOR OPENING CAUSES TIM TO SLIDE.

Tim whirls around into freezer...

Tim pushes hard to close freezer door...

Tim whirls around...
...into freezer & starts to slip on floor...

CONT'D - LEX CHARGES INTO SCENE. AND HELPS CLOSE DOOR...

CLOSE ON TIM'S FEET SLIPPING ON FLOOR.

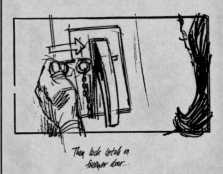

They lock latch on freezer door...

C.U. Raptor watches Tim & Lex get away...

The Raptor reacts

WIDE TO TIM & LEX THEY MAKE A BREAK FOR IT.

DOLLY. WITH TIM & LEX

DOLLY WITH TIM & LEX AS THEY .....

RUN. LOOKING OVER THEIR SHOULDERS. TO .....

LEX SLAMMING INTO A FIGURE ..... THEN.

GRANT LOWERS INTO FRAME. "ARE YOU TWO OK"

FINALE IN THE ROTUNDA

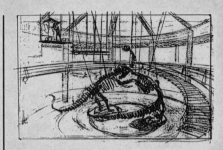

ELLIE JUMPS TO THE LAST SCAFFOLD

O.S. THEY HEAR A SHRIEK PAN OFF SLIGHTLY...

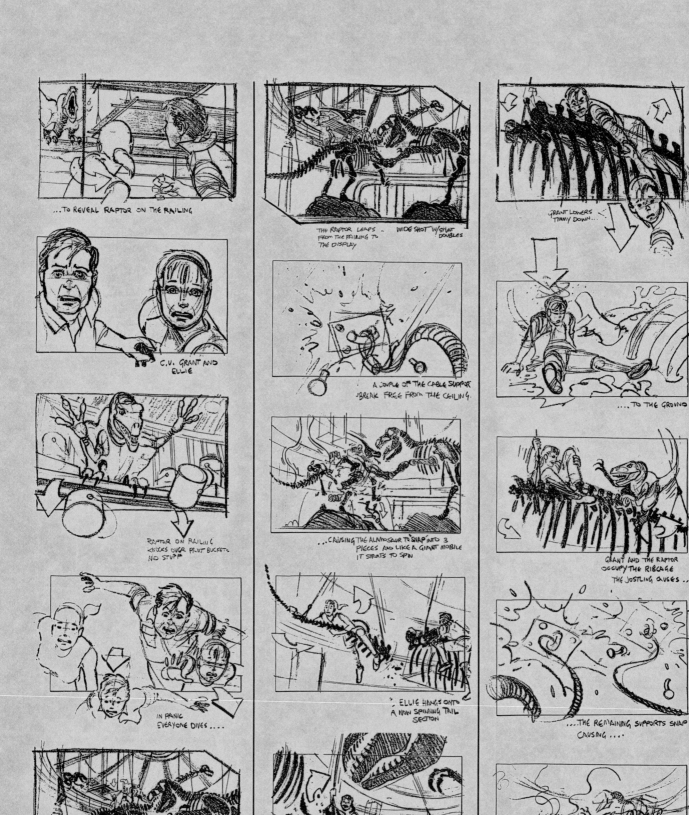

...TO REVEAL RAPTOR ON THE RAILING

THE RAPTOR LEAPS FROM THE RAILING TO THE DISPLAY — WIDE SHOT W/STUNT DOUBLES

GRANT LOWERS TIMMY DOWN...

C.U. GRANT AND ELLIE

A COUPLE OF THE CABLE SUPPORTS BREAK FREE FROM THE CEILING.

....TO THE GROUND

RAPTOR ON RAILING KNOCKS OVER PAINT BUCKETS AND STUFF

...CAUSING THE ALAMOSAUR TO SNAP INTO 3 PIECES AND LIKE A GIANT MOBILE IT STARTS TO SPIN

GRANT AND THE RAPTOR OCCUPY THE RIBCAGE THE JOSTLING CAUSES ...

IN PANIC EVERYONE DIVES ....

ELLIE HANGS ONTO A NOW SPINNING TAIL SECTION

....THE REMAINING SUPPORTS SNAP CAUSING ....

...ONTO THE SKELETON DISPLAY — WIDE SHOT W/STUNT DOUBLES

LEX CLINGS TO THE ALAMO NECK SECTION

.....THE ENTIRE ALAMOSAUR SKELETON COLLAPSES PEOPLE GET THROWN TO THE GROUND

GRANT HITS THE GROUND
AMIDST ALL THE BONES

ELLIE HITS
HARD...

AND LEX

GRANT + CO. START TO
RUN OUT OF THE V.C.
...

THE SILOUETTE OF RAPTOR #2 BEHIND
VISQUEEN

STOPS OUR GANG IN THEIR
TRACKS

C.V. OF RAPTOR BEHIND
VISQUEEN...

THEN IT TEARS THRU

OUR GANG CAUGHT IN
THE MIDDLE

THEY RAPIDLY LOOK
BACK AND FORTH BETWEEN
THE RAPTORS

O.S. WE HEAR A HUGE SMASH,
CRUNCH!
A SHADOW WIPES UP OUR
GANG....

...THEY LOOK BACK TO SEE...

RAPTOR #2 CHARGES GRANT + CO.

THE RAPTOR LEAPS AND IN MID.
AIR IT......

...THE REX GRABS IT IN ITS
MOUTH

O.S. WE HEAR A SHREK! GRANT TURNS TO SEE....

PAN W/ACTION PAST GRANT + KIDS. THE RAPTOR LEAPS.

ONTO THE NECK OF THE T-REX SINKING IT'S FANGS AND CLAWS INTO IT

WITH SHADOWS DESCRIBING THE ACTION, GRANT AND THE KIDS.

....TAKE OFF

GRANT GO!

THE REX DROPS RAPTOR #1 AS SHE FLAILS AROUND WITH RAPTOR #2 ON HER NECK

THE REX VIOLENTLY SHAKES IT'S HEAD TO LOOSEN THE CLINGING RAPTOR

THE REX FLINGS THE RAPTOR INTO THE REX SKELETON SMASHING IT TO BITS

THE REX INSPECTS THE FALLEN RAPTOR ....

...THEN ROARS IN VICTORY

FILM CREDITS

PRODUCTION STAFF

Directed by ....STEVEN SPIELBERG
Screenplay by ....MICHAEL CRICHTON and DAVID KOEPP
Based on the novel by ....MICHAEL CRICHTON
Produced by.................KATHLEEN KENNEDY, GERALD R. MOLEN
SAM NEILL
LAURA DERN
JEFF GOLDBLUM
and RICHARD ATTENBOROUGH as JOHN HAMMOND
BOB PECK
MARTIN FERRERO
B.D. WONG
SAMUEL L. JACKSON
WAYNE KNIGHT
JOSEPH MAZZELLO
ARIANA RICHARDS
Director of Photography....................................DEAN CUNDEY, A.S.C.
Production Designer...RICK CARTER
Film Edited by...MICHAEL KAHN, A.C.E.
Music by...JOHN WILLIAMS
Associate Producers ....LATA RYAN, COLIN WILSON
Unit Production Manager...PAUL DEASON
First Assistant Director.......................................JOHN T. KRETCHMER
Second Assistant Director ....MICHELE PANELLI-VENETIS
Full-Motion Dinosaurs By ....DENNIS MUREN A.S.C.
Live Action Dinosaurs.....................................STAN WINSTON
Dinosaur Supervisor ....PHIL TIPPETT
Special Dinosaur Effects.....................................MICHAEL LANTIERI
Casting by.......JANET HIRSHENSON, C.S.A., JANE JENKINS, C.S.A.
Art Directors.......................................JIM TEEGARDEN, JOHN BELL
Set Decorator ....JACKIE CARR
Stunt Coordinator..GARY HYMES
Camera Operator.......................................RAYMOND STELLA
Sound Mixer...RON JUDKINS
Paleontologist Consultant ....JACK HORNER
First Assistant Camera ....CAL ROBERTS
Second Assistant Camera ....JOLANDA WIPFLI
Loader...STEVE SFETKU
Still Photographer ....MURRAY CLOSE
Boom Operator...BOB JACKSON
Cable Operator ....TOVE BLUE VALENTINE
Video Engineer ....IAN KELLY
Script Supervisor ....ANA MARIA QUINTANA
Women's Costume Supervisor ....SUE MOORE
Men's Costume Supervisor ....ERIC SANDBERG
Costumers ....KELLY PORTER, MITCH KENNEY
Textile Artist ....PHYLLIS THURBER-MOFFIT
Property Master...JERRY MOSS
Assistant Property Masters.............KEN PETERSON, CRAIG RAICHE
Second Second Assistant Director ....KENNETH J. SILVERSTEIN
DGA Trainee..FRED ROTH
Unit Publicist...MARSHA ROBERTSON

Production Office Coordinator ....ANGELA HEALD
Assistant Production Coordinator.......................SHERRY MARSHALL
Production Secretary ....LYNNE CANNIZZARO
Make-up Supervisor ....CHRISTINA SMITH
Assistant Make-up Supervisor...........................MONTY WESTMORE
Body Make-up..JULIE STEFFES
Hair Supervisor ....LYNDA GURASICH
Assistant Hair Supervisor ....FRIDA ARADOTTIR
Chief Lighting Technician....................................MARK WALTHOUR
Assistant Chief Lighting Technicians....................STEVE CHANDLER,
O'SHANA WALKER
Rigging Gaffer ....PAT MARSHALL
Lighting Technicians ....EDWARD THOMPSON,
ANTHONY WONG, KEITH ROVERUD, HENRY "HANK"
CHARLESTON, RON WOODSIDE, BEN O. GRAHAM
Key Grip ....RON CARDARELLI
Best Boy Grips ....SID LUCERO
Dolly Grip,...DAVID WACHTMAN
Key Rigging Grip ....BUD HELLER
Grips ....STEVE CARDARELLI, MARTY DOBKOUSKY,
MICHAEL R. HEATH, BILL VENEGAS, JOHN O'GRADY,
JOHN COKER
Special Effects Foreman ....DON ELLIOT
Special Effects Shop Supervisor ....TOM PAHK
Special Effects Engineer ....JOSS GEIDUSCHEK
Special Effects ....STEVE BUNYEA, BRUCE MINKUS,
KIM DERRY, MARK T. NOEL, CORY FAUCHER,
DANIEL OSSELLO, ERIK HARALSTED, JON PORTER,
TERRY W. KING, E. WAYNE RABOUIN, LOUIE LANTIERI,
BRIAN TIPTON, MATTHEW J. McDONNEL
Special Effects Rigging Foreman ....TIM MORAN
Assistant Art Directors....................LAUREN CORY, MARTY KLINE,
PAUL SONSKI
Set Designers.........................JOHN BERGER, MASAKO MASUDA,
LAUREN POLIZZI
Chief Sculptor ....YAREK ALFER
Illustrators ....TOM CRANHAM, DAVID LOWERY
Computer Design ....STEFAN DECHANT
Art Dept. Coordinator...CAROLINE QUINN
Leadman ....TIM DONELAN
Swing Gang ....SCOTT LESLIE
Location Manager ....STUART NEUMANN
Casting Associate..MICHAEL HIRSHENSON
Casting Assistant ....SUSANNA GRIFFITH
Extras Casting..CENTRAL CASTING
Construction Coordinator ....JOHN VILLARINO
Construction Foreman...........MIKE VILLARINO, DAN PEMBERTON,
JOHN ELLIOTT
Head Paint Foreman...PAT GOMES
Paint Foreman...............................NANCY GOMES, TOM HRUPCHO,
DAVE TREEVINO
Stand-by Painter...TONY LEONARDI

Tool Foreman ....ANTHONY FEOLA
Head Laborer ....BRIAN ROCK
Plaster Foreman ....DAVID ROBBIE
Head Greensman...DANNY ONDREJKO
Greens Foreman ....KEVIN MAGNAN
Greensmen ....JEFF BROWN, BOB SKEMP, HUGO HERRERA
Craft Service ....TIM GONZALES
Display Graphics Supervisor ....MICHAEL BACKES
Display Graphics ....DAVID NAKABAYASHI
24 Frame Computer Sync ....JOHN MONSOUR, BRIAN CALLIER
Assistant Editors ....ALAN CODY, PETER FANDETTI,
PATRICK CRANE
Apprentice Editor ....MICHAEL FALLAVOLITA
Dinosaur Specialists ....JOHN GURCHE, GREGORY PAUL,
MARK HALLET
Skeletal Display ....RESEARCH CASTING INTERNATIONAL
Slide Show Coordinator ....PATTI PODESTA
Goat and Body Parts ....LANCE ANDERSON
Additional Video Assist ....DEBORAH KELMAN
Production Controller.....................................JANE GOE
Production Accountant ....JIM TURNER
Assistant Production Accountant ....DEBORAH HENDERSON
Construction Accountant ....KAY JORDAN
Payroll Accountant...KRISTEN NYE
Assistant Accountants ....ELENA HOLDEN, CHRISTINE STEWART
Set Dressing Coordinator.............................JANINE CAVOTO
Assistant to Mr. Spielberg ....BONNIE CURTIS
2nd Assistant to Mr. Spielberg ....KAREN BITTENSON-KUSHELL
Assistants to Ms. Kennedy ....BETH CAHN, LESLIE CHEATHAM
Assistant to Mr. Molen ....DIANA TINKLEY
Assistant to Ms. Ryan ....REBECCA CHAIRES
Assistant to Sam Neill ....SIMON MILLAR
Production Assistants ....CRAIG BARNETT, JOHN SMITH,
JOSEPH J.M. KENNY, ROBERT WEST
Transportation Coordinator...........................DENNY CAIRA
Transportation Captain...................................HAL LARY
Drivers.........................TINO CAIRA, BECKY RAICHE, DON CROW,
LEROY REED, JAMES FREAR, STEVE SORKIN,
GORDON JERNBERG, MARK WESTCOTT, LORIN JORDAN,
WAYNE WILLIAMS, STEVE LUCE, MARK YACULLO
Animal Trainer..JULES SYLVESTER
Teacher...JUDY BROWN
Safety Coordinator ....TIM LITCHAUER
Stand-ins...............................DON FELDSTEIN, DAVIDA VACCARO,
JOHNNY JOHNSON, JOE ZIMMERMAN, CYNTHIA MADVIG
2nd Unit First Assistant Director........................CARLA McCLOSKEY
Additional Photography...................................LLOYD AHERN II
2nd Unit Gaffer..JACK SCHLOSSER
Helicopter ....BLUE HAWAIIAN HELICOPTER

HAWAII UNIT
Location Manager..KEN LEVINE
Asst. Location Manager...................................SAM LEE
Asst. Production Coordinator...........................VICTORIA MATTSON
Office Assistant...TRACI TATEYAMA
Transportation Captain....................................HARRY UESHIRO
Grip ....RUBEN VASQUEZ

Electric..ROGER THOMPSON
Security ....MARK TRAVIS
Extras Casting...SHOWLITES

AERIAL UNIT
Aerial Unit Director ....DAVID NOWELL
Aerial Coordinator ....BOBBY ZAJONC
Assistant Camera..JOHN CONNELL
Picture Pilot ....DAVID CHEVALIER
Safety Coordinator ....CYNTHIA ZAJONC

"MR. D.N.A." ANIMATION
Animation by ....KURTZ AND FRIENDS
Movement Design..BOB KURTZ
Layout Design ....ROBERT PELUCE

FULL MOTION DINOSAURS AND SPECIAL VISUAL EFFECTS
BY INDUSTRIAL LIGHT & MAGIC
A Division of Lucas Digital Ltd.
Co-Visual Effects Supervisor ....MARK A. Z. DIPPÉ
Visual Effects Producer ....JANET HEALY
Lead Computer Graphics Supervisor ....STEFEN M. FANGMEIER
Computer Graphics Supervisors ...ALEX SEIDEN, GEORGE MURPHY
ILM General Manager......................................JIM MORRIS
Computer Graphics Animators.............................ERIC ARMSTRONG,
JAMES SATORU STRAUS, STEVE SPAZ WILLIAMS,
GEOFF CAMPBELL, STEVE PRICE, DON WALLER
Computer Graphics Artists ....JEAN M. CUNNINGHAM,
JOSEPH PASQUALE, CARL N. FREDERICK, ELLEN POON,
THOMAS L. HUTCHINSON, STEVEN ROSENBAUM,
JOE LETTERI, JOHN SCHLAG, JEFFREY B. LIGHT, TIEN
TRUONG, JAMES D. MITCHELL, WADE HOWIE
Executive in Charge of Production.............................PATRICIA BLAU
Supervisor of Software and Digital Technology ....THOMAS A.
WILLIAMS
Computer Graphics Software Developers ....MICHAEL J. NATKIN,
ERIC ENDERTON, ZORAN KAČIĆ-ALESIĆ,
JOHN HORN, BRIAN KNEP, PAUL ASHDOWN
Visual Effects Coordinator ....JUDITH WEAVER
Visual Effects Art Director ....TYRUBEN ELLINGSTON
Visual Effects Editor ....MICHAEL GLEASON
Scanning Supervisor ....JOSHUA PINES
Optical Supervisor..JOHN ELLIS
Plate Photography Camera Assistant ....PATRICK McCARDLE
ILM Plate Producer ....MARK MILLER
Digital Artists.................................CAROLYN ENSLE RENDU,
BART GIOVANNETTI, DAVID CARSON, RITA E. ZIMMERMAN,
SANDY HOUSTON, KATHLEEN BEELER, BARBARA BRENNAN,
GREG MALONEY, LISA DROSTOVA
Computer Graphics Camera Matchmovers ....PATRICK T. MYERS,
CHARLIE CLAVADETSCHER
Computer Graphics Technical Assistants ....STEVE MOLIN,
MICHAEL CONTE, JOEL ARON, CURT I. MIYASHIRO,
EDWIN DUNKLEY, PATRICK NEARY
Scanning Operators.................................RANDALL K. BEAN,
GEORGE GAMBETTA, MIKE ELLIS
Computer Graphics Systems Support................................KEN BEYER,
LINDA J. SEIGEL, JAY LENCI

Video Engineers...................................FRED MEYERS, GARY MEYER
Computer Graphics Coordinators.............................GINGER THEISEN,
NANCY JILL LUCKOFF
CG Department Production Manager.............................GAIL CURREY
CG Department Operations Manager....JOHN ANDREW BERTON, JR.
Senior CG Department Manager.......................DOUGLAS SCOTT KAY
Visual Effects Camera Operators..PAT TURNER, TERRY CHOSTNER
Additional Plate Photography.......................................SCOTT FARRAR
Camera Assistants...............................ROBERT HILL, JEFF GREELEY
Matte Artists........................CHRISTOPHER EVANS, YUSEI UESUGI
Assistant Editor...ROBERTO McGRATH
Negative Cutter...LOUIS RIVERA
Projectionist.......................................TIMOTHY A. GREENWOOD
Editorial Coordinator...DAVID TANAKA
Chief Model Makers.......BARBARA AFFONSO, LORNE PETERSON,
STEVE GAWLEY, IRA KEELER, CHRISTOPHER REED
Stage Technicians...........PAT FITZSIMMONS, TIMOTHY MORGAN,
ROBERT FINLEY, JR., WILLIAM BARR
Optical Camera Operators.....................................KEITH L. JOHNSON,
JAMES C. LIM
Optical Line Up.............JOHN D. WHISNANT, KRISTEN TRATTNER
Optical Lab Technician...TIM GEIDEMAN
Optical/Scanning Coordinator...LISA VAUGHN
Camera Engineers.............DUNCAN SUTHERLAND, MIKE BOLLES
Production Accountant..PAMELA KAY
Courier Coordinator..JERRY SIMONSEN
Production Assistant..TINA MATTHIES

STAN WINSTON STUDIO
Art Department Coordinators JOHN ROSENGRANT, SHANE MAHAN
Mechanical Department Coordinators...................RICHARD LANDON,
CRAIG CATON-LARGENT
Concept Artist...MARK "CRASH" McCREERY
Mechanical Design...............CHARLES LUTKUS III, RICH HAUGEN,
EVAN BRAINARD, RICHARD GALINSON, TIM NORDELLA,
ALFRED SOUSA, JEFF EDWARDS, JON DAWE,
PATRICK SHEARN, J. ALAN SCOTT
Technical Coordinator T-Rex..CRAIG BARR
Hydraulic Engineer...LLOYD BALL
Master Welder...ARMANDO GONZALEZ
Key Artists...MIKE TRCIC, SHANNON SHEA,
CHRISTOPHER SWIFT, DAVE GRASSO, JOEY OROSCO,
ROB HINDERSTEIN, ANDY SCHONEBERG, JOSEPH READER,
GREG FIGIEL, IAN STEVENSON, BILL BASSO, PAUL MEJIAS
Master Mold Maker...ANTHONY McCRAY
Dinosaur Skin Fabricators.................................RICHARD DAVISON,
MARILYN DOZER-CHANEY, KAREN MASON
Art Department..........................BETH HATHAWAY, NICK MARRA,
MICHIKO TAGAWA, ROBERT RAMSDELL, DAVID BENEKE,
SCOTT "GWIDGE" URBAN, MARK JURINKO,
FRANCESCA AVILA, MITCH COUGHLIN,
SEBASTIN CAILLABET, NATHALIE FRATTI-RAPOPORT,
ANTHONY GAILLARD, LINDSAY McGOWAN,
PIERRE OLIVIER THEUENIN, JEFF PERIERA, LEN BURGE,
KEVIN McTURK, EILEEN KASTNER-DELAGO, ERIC OSTROFF,
KEVIN WILLIS, BRAD KRISKO, ADAM JONES
Mechanical Department.............BRIAN NAMANNY, BRUCE STARK,
MATT DURHAM, GREGORY MANION

Production Coordinators..........................TARA MEANEY-CROCITTO,
MARK LOHFF
Production Assistants.......CHUCK ZLOTNICK, KIMBERLY VERROS

TIPPETT STUDIO
Production Supervisor..JULES TIPPETT
Computer Interface Engineer...CRAIG HAYES
Senior Animator..RANDAL M. DUTRA
Animator..TOM ST. AMAND
Computer Systems...ADAM VALDEZ
Production Coordinator...SHEILA DUIGNAN
Production.................SUZANNE NIKI YOSHII, REBECCA SCHIROS
Engineering...............................NICHOLAS BLAKE, BART TRICKEL,
CONRAD BONDERSON, GARY PLATEK, STUART ZIFF
Animatics..................................ERIC SWENSON, MIKE BIENSTOCK,
KIM BLANCHETTE, PETER KONIG
Computer Technicians....................STEVE REDING, DOUGLAS EPPS

Post production sound services provided by
Skywalker Sound, a division of
Lucas Digital LTD.
Marin County, California

Re-Recording Mixers............GARY SUMMERS, GARY RYDSTROM,
SHAWN MURPHY
Sound Design...GARY RYDSTROM
Supervising Sound Editor.......................................RICHARD HYMNS
Sound Effect Editors...........................KEN FISCHER, TIM HOLLAND,
TERRY ECKTON
ADR Editor..LAUREL LADEVICH
Dialogue Editors.......................MICHAEL SILVERS, SARA BOLDER
Foley Editors....SANDINA BAILO-LAPE, MARY HELEN LEASMAN
Asst. Supv. Sound Editor..RUTH HASTY
Assistant Sound Designer...CHRIS BOYES
Assistant Sound Effects Editors......J. R. GRUBBS, SCOTT GUITTEAU
Assistant ADR Editor..BOB MARTY
Assistant Dialogue Editors....................DONNA JAFFE, MAIA VERES
Assistant Foley Editor..SUSAN POPOVICH
Apprentice Editor..ANDRE FENLEY
Foley Artists..............................DENNIE THORPE, MARNIE MOORE
Foley Recordist..CHRIS BOYES

Music Editor...KENNETH WANNBERG
Music Contractor...SANDY DECRESCENT
Music Preparation............................JO ANN KANE MUSIC SERVICE
Music Scoring Mixer..SHAWN MURPHY
Scoring Crew.......................SUSAN McCLEAN, MARK ESHELMAN,
GREG DENNEN, RICHARD DEARMAS, BILL TALBOT
Orchestrations...............JOHN NEUFELD, ALEXANDER COURAGE
Post Production Assistant...ROBERT WEST
ADR Mixer..DEAN DRABIN
ADR Recordist..ANN HASDELL
ADR Re-Recorded At.................TODD-AO/GLEN GLEN STUDIOS
ADR Voice Casting...BARBARA HARRIS
Music Recorded at......................................SONY PICTURES STUDIOS
Color Timers..................................DALE CALDWELL, ART HALISSI
Negative Cutter...GARY BURRITT
Amblin Projectionist...RENE GONZALEZ

Dolby Stereo Consultant.................................DOUGLAS GREENFIELD
Titles and Opticals by...PACIFIC TITLE
Remote Control Camera Systems by............NETTMANN/MATTHEWS
Process Compositing by...HANSARD
Crane and Dollies by ....CHAPMAN
Gyrosphere by.....................................PRESTON CAMERA SYSTEMS

CAST

Grant ....SAM NEILL
Ellie ....LAURA DERN
Malcolm ....JEFF GOLDBLUM
Hammond...RICHARD ATTENBOROUGH
Muldoon...BOB PECK
Gennaro...MARTIN FERRERO
Wu...B.D. WONG
Tim..JOSEPH MAZZELLO
Lex...ARIANA RICHARDS
Arnold..SAMUEL L. JACKSON
Nedry ....WAYNE KNIGHT
Harding ....JERRY MOLEN
Rostagno..MIGUEL SANDOVAL
Dodgson..CAMERON THOR
Volunteer #1 ....CHRISTOPHER JOHN FIELDS
Volunteer Boy...WHIT HERTFORD
Mate..DEAN CUNDEY
Worker in Raptor pen ....JOPHERY BROWN
Helicopter Pilot ....TOM MISHLER
"Mr. D.N.A." Voice ....GREG BURSON
Worker at Amber Mine ....ADRIAN ESCOBER
Jurassic Park Tour Voice ....RICHARD KILEY

PUPPETEERS

LLOYD BALL	SHANE MAHAN
CRAIG BARR	KAREN MASON
BILL BASSO	MARK "CRASH" McCREERY
DAVID BENEKE	PAUL MEJIAS
LARRY BOLSTER	TIM NORDELLA
EVAN BRAINARD	JOEY OROSCO
CRAIG CATON	JEFF PERIERA
MITCH COUGHLIN	JOSEPH READER
RICHARD DAVISON	JOHN ROSENGRANT
JON DAWE	ANDY SCHONEBERG
JEFF EDWARDS	J. ALAN SCOTT
GREG FIGIEL	SHANNON SHEA
RICK GALINSON	PATRICK SHEARN
ARMONDO GONZALEZ	ALFRED SOUSA
AVE GRASSO	IAN STEVENSON
BETH HATHAWAY	CHRISTOPHER SWIFT
RICHARD HAUGEN	MICHIKO TAGAWA
RICHARD LANDON	MIKE TRCIC
CHARLES LUTKUS III	MATT WINSTON

STUNTS

NATALIE BOLINGER	GARY EPPER
LAURA DASH	DONNA EVANS
RUSTY HANSON	LARRY DAVIS
NORMAN HOWELL	GARY McCLARTY
LES LARSON	PAT ROMANO
BRIAN SMRZ	R.A. RONDELL
PATRICK TALLMAN	

Filmed at
Universal Studios and
Kauai, Hawaii

The Producers Wish to Thank the Following:
GEORGE LUCAS
THE ISLAND & PEOPLE OF KAUAI—MAYOR JOANN YUKIMORA
KAUAI FILM COMMISSIONER JUDY DROSD
STATE OF HAWAII FILM OFFICE
CALIFORNIA FILM COMMISSION
IRIS INDIGO ELANS AND 4D/440 VGXT COMPUTER SYSTEMS
PROVIDED BY SILICON GRAPHICS
APPLE COMPUTER, INC.
SUPERMAC TECHNOLOGY
3D WEATHER SOFTWARE BY EARTHWATCH
COMMUNICATIONS MINNEAPOLIS
4D CREATIVE ENVIRONMENT PROVIDED BY SOFTIMAGE
ELECTRIC IMAGE
NEWER TECHNOLOGY
KAIMBU ISLAND RESORT, FIJI
TURTLE ISLAND, FIJI
TROPICALS BY GORDON COURTRIGHT © 1988, BY
TIMBER PRESS
RIXAN & ASSOCIATES, INC.
GENETIC ENGINEERING NEWS, MARY ANN LEIBERT, INC.
PUBLISHERS
CARL ZEISS, INC.
HELICOPTER TOUR OPERATORS OF KAUAI
THE DINOSAUR SOCIETY-DON LESSEM
CONNECTION MACHINE (CM-5) SUPERCOMPUTER SYSTEM
BY THINKING MACHINES CORPORATION

"QUB MILAGRO CHAPPARITA"
Written by Dolores Ayala Olivares
Performed by Madacy Mariachi Bond
Courtesy of Madacy Music Group

ORIGINAL SOUNDTRACK ON MCA CDS AND CASSETTES

THIS FILM MIXED AND RECORDED IN A THX SOUND SYSTEM
THEATRE

FILMED WITH PANAVISION CAMERA & LENSES

Color by DELUXE

DOLBY STEREO
in Selected Theaters

THIS FILM MIXED AND RECORDED IN A THX SOUND SYSTEM
THEATRE
EASTMAN COLOR FILM
DIGITAL THEATRE SYSTEM

CERTIFICATE NO	IATSE
MPAA SEAL	INSIGNIA

A STEVEN SPIELBERG FILM

AMBLIN ENTERTAINMENT

MPAA CODE Classification

Standard Universal Studios Logo

Standard Tour Log

ABOUT THE AUTHORS

Don Shay is founder and publisher of *Cinefex* magazine. Jody Duncan is editor of the same publication. Both have written extensively on motion pictures and effects technology; and, as collaborators, they have produced books on the making of *Ghostbusters* and *Terminator 2*. Shay has contributed video interviews to recent laserdisc supplements for *Close Encounters of the Third Kind, Alien* and *Aliens.* Duncan is an award-winning playwright whose *A Warring Absence* was honored last year at the Kennedy Center in Washington, D.C.